ENID BAGNOLD

(1889-1981), was the daughter of Ethel Alger and Arthur Henry Bagnold, a professional soldier. Born at Rochester, she spent some childhood years in Jamaica. At the age of nineteen, "finished, burnished, ready", Enid Bagnold moved to Chelsea with a yearly allowance of seventy five pounds and became a student at Walter Sickert's drawing school. She then worked briefly for Frank Harris as a "sort of" journalist.

At the outbreak of war Enid Bagnold became a VAD nurse at the Royal Herbert Hospital, Woolwich: *A Diary Without Dates* (1917) recounts her experiences there. The book made national headlines and secured her instant dismissal. Later, as one of the First Aid Nursing Yeomanry, she served in France as a driver, providing material for her first novel, *The Happy Foreigner* (1920). In the same year Enid Bagnold married Sir Roderick Jones, Chairman of Reuters, with whom she had three sons and a daughter. As Lady Jones, she spent much time as a hostess but preserved three hours a day for writing. Her friends included Gaudier Brzeska, Lovat Fraser, Ralph Hodgson, Prince Antoine Bibesco, H. G. Wells, Vita Sackville-West, Harold Nicolson, Lady Diana Cooper and Rudyard Kipling.

Enid Bagnold's second novel, *Serena Blandish*, appeared in 1924, published pseudonymously to spare the embarrassment of Colonel Bagnold. Other novels are: *Alice and Thomas and Jane* (1930), a children's book; the world famous *National Velvet* (1935), later successfully staged and filmed; *The Squire* (1938); and *The Loved and Envied* (1951). She was also a distinguished playwright. Her nine plays include: *Lottie Dundass* (1943), *The Chalk Garden* (1956) also filmed; and *The Chinese Prime Minister* (1964). Enid Bagnold's *Autobiography* was published in 1969 and in 1976 she was made a Commander of the British Empire. She lived at Rottingdean, Sussex—in a house previously owned by Burne-Jones—until her death.

The Squire

ENID BAGNOLD

WITH A NEW INTRODUCTION BY
ANNE SEBBA

PENGUIN BOOKS – VIRAGO PRESS

PENGUIN BOOKS

Viking Penguin Inc., 40 West 23rd Street,
New York, New York 10010, U.S.A.
Penguin Books Ltd, Harmondsworth,
Middlesex, England
Penguin Books Australia Ltd, Ringwood,
Victoria, Australia
Penguin Books Canada Limited, 2801 John Street,
Markham, Ontario, Canada L3R 1B4
Penguin Books (N.Z.) Ltd, 182–190 Wairau Road,
Auckland 10, New Zealand

First published in Great Britain by Wm. Heinemann 1938
This edition first published in Great Britain by Virago Press Limited 1987
Published in Penguin Books 1987

Printed in Finland
by Werner Söderström Oy

INTRODUCTION

Harold Nicolson once compared Enid Bagnold's talent with a slowly dripping tap. "Your sort of writing *ought* to drip rather than to splash," he told her when she complained to him about the small volume of her literary output. "The quality of your drops is such that the quantity does not matter in the least." Eventually, he reassured her, a basin would be filled with carefully distilled water.

The Squire, written over a period of some fifteen years, unquestionably fell into the category of distilled writing. From 1921, when her first child was born, until 1930 when her fourth and last arrived, she made extensive notes on her experiences of childbirth and of motherhood. Later, as she watched the gradual loosening of maternal ties she realised that she wanted to write not only about birth but also to explore in detail the intimate and growing relationship between the mother and her family. This, she believed, had never before been attempted in a novel. Most importantly, she wished to describe her own attitudes towards middle age with respect to sex and the family. But, although always described as a novel, the serious effort to discover the motivations of a mother and the instincts of children leads *The Squire* close to the realms of documentary.

The "story" begins with the entry of a midwife into a well-to-do country household teeming with children and servants, a few days before the birth of the fifth child. The husband has departed on a three-month business trip to Bombay and does not appear throughout the book. From this time the woman is referred to only as "the squire", the Begum of this masterless house. Enid's own husband often spent the entire week in London, alone, returning only at weekends. In 1926 he had been preparing for a long business trip which would have taken him away before the birth of his third child. In the event he was delayed by the General Strike and left shortly after the baby had arrived. But Enid realised more clearly than ever after this that men were not necessary for the busy domestic routine which is the book's backdrop.

She who had once been thirsty and gay, square-shouldered, fair and military, strutting about life for spoil, was thickened now, vigorous, leonine, occupied with her house, her nursery, her servants, her knot of human lives, antagonistic or loving . . . she was well-accustomed to . . . her own supreme command.

Thus wrote Enid Bagnold about a character more completely herself than any other she had yet created. But although the description of vigour and healthfulness well fitted her, in reality she retained more feminine charm and allure than she allowed her fictional heroine. The squire, we are told, had once been intensely female to her lovers, "but now what was left standing at the core was the rock of neutral human stuff, neither male nor female".

Apart from this masculine, commanding streak in the squire herself, men are deliberately eliminated from the book. Instead, life centres on a small, tightly-knit circle of women, the English Harem as the author once called it. Enid was matriarch in her own family—both the dispenser of punishments and the provider of fun. The squire was cast in the same mould.

Men, accepted as necessary for procreation, are introduced to the book through Caroline, the squire's aristocratic friend and neighbour. This woman, younger and more attractive, is pursued by men. At the moment she has a lover in Paris and arrives one day for lunch to discuss the affair. Although Caroline, loosely based on Enid's friend Lady Cynthia Asquith, is the squire's foil, the conversation between them is more a study of one woman at two different periods of her life. "That lovely creature is my youth!" reflects the squire.

As the squire listens to the dramas of Caroline's life she hears nothing but empty words, devoid of any real meaning or significance. This helps her realise that she is now ready to live without the pain of sexual love. She is "saying farewell to sex ... looking to a future in which I shall find again what life is made of, bare life, without mirage, without props". Men can no longer light her up, as they once had, only the baby does that now. When he is taken away the light goes out of the room. By contrast, Caroline's complicated tale of love appears to the mother "indescribably stale".

The discussions with Caroline have a positively liberating effect on the squire by making her come to terms with her age (forty-four) and recognise that she is no longer dependent on men acting as her alcohol and stimulant. She is finding middle age un-expectedly enjoyable. "There is a kind of savage joy in getting to the end of the pleasures of youth," she explains. "After forty the sense of beauty grows less acute; one is troubled instead by a vast organ note, a hum of death." Comforted by the knowledge that her own "lover" is "in her lap", can she sit patiently hearing out the agonies of Caroline's imbroglio.

The squire refers to Caroline as a "love-woman", the sort of woman men have in mind in using the term woman. But she and her type ought to be called by a different name. "Wumen", the author proposes. "Wumen are hard-working, faulty, honest, female males." There is a third type of woman in *The Squire*, personified by the midwife. "You and those like you have become a third sex." This character was inspired by Enid's own midwife, Ethel Raynham Smith, a frail but fiery-looking redhead. Raynham Smith was driven by the conviction that, if the conditions of birth were correct, it would be possible to create a healthier race. Enid, because she combined intelligence with a willingness to comply with the midwife's strictures, endeared herself to Nurse Raynham Smith in a way no man ever could. She not only loved Enid, she sometimes experienced "a mystical rare link with you that will carry on for ever". Enid was aware of Nurse Raynham Smith's power. "In me she set up an excitement, an anticipation of the event, a desire to produce a wonderful child that exceeded anything I had ever been told about my private health and private future. Her serene and bright spirit entered my life and, sword in hand, entered my house."

The squire's midwife, too, is both fierce and ascetic, a soldier fighting for the birth to go smoothly and uninterrupted. To her "it was the prince arriving; core and stomach of her work, leap and triumph of her virgin maternity". She tells the squire: "I am virginal and narrow but I am his gardener." The thoughts belong to Raynham Smith but their poetic expression is Bagnold. Men, or rather husbands, the nurse openly admits, are a hindrance to her work; only her partner, the doctor, is an exception: the monk and the nun, the squire calls this pair. The midwife prepares the household for the tremendous events of the birth, the reader for the climax of the novel. Recognising her temporary ascendancy, the squire lets her take over for a short time.

INTRODUCTION

The children, however, are the book's
mainspring. Enid had, through her member-
ship of the Chelsea Babies Club and by letters
to *The Times* about the care and well-being of
children and babies, acquired a reputation as
something of an expert on child welfare. None
the less, children in general left her unmoved.
"How dull are the faces of children who are
not mine," she wrote in *The Squire*. It was the
belief in her own children's superiority which
moved her so intensely. Vita Sackville-West
noticed this and told Enid she was "a prig
about being a mother", an allegation she did
not entirely refute. To another friend Enid
asserted: "You do not know what it is fully to
be a woman until you've had at least three
children ... and I am having four." The fifth
child in *The Squire* was purely imaginary. The
squire, as she watches her children, "burned
with pride, inwardly shaken with wonder ...
see how magnificently now they walked up the
street".

Not surprisingly, the children are most
accurately and lovingly observed, although

Jay, the eldest boy, is rather sketchily drawn.
The reader is told little more than that he has
"a sweet face, light hair turning brown ...
arrogance, flushing tempers, pride and reasonableness". The picture of his younger brother,
Boniface, is fuller. He is:

red of face, asking no help, intent upon some inner
life which would not swim up into his difficult
speech. Boniface unhelpable, resolved to lead the
life of a man before he was fit to leave babyhood
for childhood. Inarticulate, eccentric, living like a
mole in his world, putting into dangerous
execution plans to which no one had the key.

If the squire admitted to any pain it would be
because she found Boniface "unhelpable".
Henry, based on Enid's own youngest, was a

creature like a resolute angel that ran naked in the
garden in the summer, with dirty feet that picked
up leaves with the toes ... [He] was filled with
desire from top to toe ... with a wild lust for
possession ... cloaked in beauty.

The squire has a special relationship with
Lucy, the only daughter, who takes so much

responsibility on her own shoulders and tries
to save Boniface from getting into trouble
because she finds him "touching and divine".
Just as Caroline is the squire as a young
woman, Lucy portrays her as a girl. The
squire, believing she is one in a line of women,
her mother before her, the child Lucy behind,
takes "a stoic pleasure in *procession*". She has
formed several images of this procession. At
one moment she sees herself as "a pipe
through which the generations pass". At
another she felt like "an archway through
which her children flowed; and cared less that
the clock in the arch's crown ticked Time
away". In a third processional image she sees
herself as one in a line of "Greek women in
fluttering robes rounding a vase's girth for
ever". When she tells Lucy never to feel
indebted or guilty towards her it is because
"to have a child is an account which is settled
on the spot ... love me but don't be grateful
... what I do for you I do for myself!"

There are almost as many reflections on
death as on birth in the book as the life cycle is

an ever-present reality for the squire. The realisation that she would not always be alive to protect her children had once been almost unendurable. Only this vision of immortality through her children was comforting.

The squire spends the hours before the birth not only ruminating on her children and the nature of humanity in general but also in trying to engage a new cook. Finally she is ready to let birth be the sole invader of her thoughts. But she does not worry either about the danger to herself (a fear which most forty-year-olds in 1938 could not ignore) nor is she apprehensive about labour pains. She tells Caroline, who listens aghast, that she has learned how to deal with the convulsions. Pain, if it is not resisted, is just another branch of sensation, she explains.

There comes a time, after the first pains have passed, when you swim down a silver river running like a torrent, with the convulsive, corkscrew movements of a great fish, threshing from its neck to its tail. And if you can *marry* the movements, go with them, turn like a screw in the river and swim on ... then I believe the pain ... becomes a flame which doesn't burn you.

Enid did not deny that there was pain in childbirth. But she knew that fear (of the unknown) led to tension and compounded it. Conversely, understanding the spasms, swimming with them, lessened but did not altogether remove them. Only thus could giving birth become enjoyable. Interestingly, the squire is not given any drugs during the labour or birth, just "a touch of anaesthetic from a gauze mask". Only after, and then not to make the pain supportable, but because she was twitching with excitement and could not sleep, does she submit to a quarter of morphine.

At this time, when a woman had little information to alleviate her fears apart from Dr Grantly Dick Read's sober *Natural Childbirth* (1933) Bagnold's was a daring approach to an almost taboo subject. Contemporary reviewers on the whole heaped praise on the work. But such a frank discussion of birth and breast-feeding, although characteristic of the author's courage and forthrightness, was not universally welcomed. Some of her friends, even in other respects advanced thinkers, considered her outspokenness shocking, particularly her use of the word nipple in public. H. G. Wells said the book made him feel as if, "I'd been attacked by a multitude of many-breasted women (like Diana of Ephesus) and thrown into a washing basket full of used nursery napkins."

Fifty years later such reactions appear prudish. Today, when fathers regularly assist at a birth, and television can film a baby's arrival in graphic detail there is (and some may regret it) little or no mystery left in the birth process. In addition, the science of obstetrics has made such progress that it is possible for women to experience an almost pain-free labour with minimal risk to themselves. A further anachronism is the amount of household help available to the squire. Arguably, any woman surrounded by such a host of servants would relish an opportunity for the philosophical contemplations of birth and death. But if the paraphernalia of the birth are removed and the events of the novel seen as in a time capsule, the emotions expressed are universal. Bagnold has trapped for all time not only the intensity of a mother's love for her offspring but the extreme pain and profound excitement of the actual moment of giving birth:

Her mind went down and lived in her body, ran out of her brain and lived in her flesh. She had eyes and nose and ears and senses in her body, in her backbone, living like a spiny woodlouse, doubled in a ball, having no beginning and no end. Now the first twisting spate of pain began. Swim then, swim with it for your life. If you resist, horror and impediment! If you swim, not pain but sensation! ... Keep abreast of it, rush together, you and the violence which is also you! Wild movements, hallucinated swimming! Other things exist than pain!

The Squire was published in October 1938, just after the Munich crisis. But the threat of war had barely departed from most people's minds and Hitler, the Sudeten and War were still the most pressing topics of conversation. Charles Evans, her publisher at Heinemann, told her:

It is going to be a book that matters profoundly in the present mad world—a book that will present life's values as they really are ... never before, in twenty-six years of publishing, has the idea of a book so moved me.

Enid too, while writing *The Squire*, was deeply interested in events in Europe. With the images of birth so freshly in her mind she was struck by certain parallels with the international crisis. Any connection between *The Squire* and its hymn of praise to family life and the dogma of destruction of life inherent in Nazi doctrines is not immediately evident. But Enid viewed the various European countries as squabbling children in a nursery with France the neurotic child wanting its own way; into this nursery comes the newborn baby, Nazi Germany. Not unusually, the birth was difficult and ugly but "I love to see things born," Enid wrote in some private notes about Germany at this time. "We are afraid of Hitlerism. We see in it retrogression. I see in Nazism Birth and all the horrors and beauties of birth." Enid's belief that in any revolution blood would be shed initially but then a healthy child would emerge, is, at best, romantic and naive. With hindsight, to see Nazi Germany as such a child appears blindly cruel.

Although these views give *The Squire* an underlying if subconscious symbolism, it does not follow that Enid Bagnold was writing a political tract. But it does help to explain how she saw birth not just as the arrival of one more individual in a particular family, but as a continuing process in which beauty and ugliness mean nothing separately but are irredeemably fused as part of the whole: the life cycle of the world. Thus the child in the womb, "old as a Pharoah in its tomb", is as old as Life, as old as Time, but then grows young again to enter a new earthly phase. *The Squire* might be short on plot, but its story is the most important story every told.

Already thirty when she first became a mother, having a child was a deep surprise to Enid Bagnold. The experience fitted none of her preconceived notions. "If a man had a child and he was also a writer we should have heard a lot about it," she once commented. "I wanted *The Squire* to be exactly as objective as if a man had had a baby." It is, nevertheless, a romantic book, but toughly romantic and never sentimental. Fifteen years after *The Squire* was first published she wrote: "In many ways I think I did get it right. I am sad more people haven't read it."

Anne Sebba, Richmond, 1986

CHAPTER ONE

F ROM THE VILLAGE GREEN WHERE THE
Manor House stood, well-kept, white-
painted, the sea was hidden by the turn of
the street. The house's front, pierced with
windows, blinked as the sun sank, and on the
step of the open front door stood the butler,
Pratt, come out to breathe the evening air.

Sunset and moonrise were going on
together. The black cattle, changing fields,
drifted across the Green with gilded rumps and
silvered horns. The butler watched them,
folding his arms, his distinguished, cadaverous
face filled with habitual but not insistent
gloom.

"Quite a trip," he thought, his mind on his
master gone on his annual three months' visit
to Bombay. The Unborn for whom the house
now waited in restless suspension and slightly

growing indiscipline would be a big baby by his return.

"Sir," said his parlourmaid behind him, in the middle of drawing her hall curtains.

He turned.

"Her Ladyship wants you."

Pratt went to his lady (now the squire, the Begum of this masterless house), crossing the hall and two passages and finding her in the garden in the dying light.

The parlourmaid continued to draw her curtains, shutting out western and southern glories one by one.

"Have you arst him?" said the kitchenmaid, leaning through a baize door, half concealed by a curtain.

"Not yet."

The kitchenmaid sniffed and hung in the doorway.

"He'll be back in a tick. Gone through to the garden."

"Well . . ." said the kitchenmaid, and paused.

The parlourmaid held her hand on the curtain and waited.

"I bin and fell against the larder window," said the kitchenmaid, grinning. "The pane's out!"

"You done it! I darn't."

"Darn't what?"

"Come in that way."

"Easy as easy. You undo the latch and get in easy. The dance isn't over till two. What's it matter anyway? They can't eat you. Only sack you."

"That's all," said the parlourmaid. "They can only sack me. An' ther's places for the asking. It's the fuss I hate. Well, I'll ask him an' see."

"I'd come without 'f I were you," said the kitchenmaid, disappearing.

The last curtain was drawn, the parlourmaid had gone and the hall was empty. It smelt of greenery and flowers and polish, very still, folded for its evening, waiting for its night.

The silken horse-hair hung down from the row of Indian fly-switches attached by their ivory handles to a carved rack studded with brass. Opposite them hung the English crops, in lines upon their oak hooks. The house, now masterless for a month, was nearly, too, without a mistress, for she, its temporary squire, was heavy with child, absent in mind: she, round whom the house's life pivoted, had withdrawn the intermittent firmness of her ruling hand.

Pratt returned. Not with cat's feet that might surprise; but with a solid tread meant to warn, meant to spare him unpleasantness. Opening the front door again, his back to the cloaked, unlit hall, he regarded the crash of the sunset. So much colour and light became almost noise. So much light lit up the marks on his black clothes. They hung well—he was a tall, narrow-hipped and lantern-shouldered man—but they were soapy with age and want of care.

His hands were large and dirty, the nails broken; his face fine and gloomy. He held himself with pride and a quelling carriage, his hair curled admirably round his head—a large,

4

morose, half-tamed male animal, cynical and angry, the sunset lighting his dulled eyes and proud brow.

"Sir," said the parlourmaid again. He would have liked a little peace. Not that he was doing much with his peace for his thoughts were running vexedly on the near arrival of the midwife.

He grunted and turned.

"Nurse would like a word with you."

"I'm here," he said, "for her to come."

"She said . . . if you'd just come through the passage door. . . ."

Pratt shut and bolted his hall door without haste, then pushed the passage door which led to the nursery quarters. Nurse was waiting, full of nervous talk.

"It's my girl, Mr. Pratt. It's those trays. And more that we shall be having soon!"

Pratt belted his will tighter.

"It seems my girl's got a grumbling appendix. It's that midday tray with the two big courses. If you'd let the pantry help when there's no one extra in the dining-room. . . ."

"If your girl's got a grumbling appendix she should see to it," said Pratt in frozen tones.

"You can't do anything about it till it comes to a head."

"The nursery," said Pratt, "has always been a self-supporting unit. Once it isn't you don't know where you are."

"Have a heart, Mr. Pratt. It's to tide over. The girl's grumbling so."

Pratt knew how to refuse. He refused, closing the subject. Nurse ran, flurried, to her lady in the garden.

But the "squire" had gone. She had gathered up her sewing in the dying light. There was her chair (still depressed by her great weight), her back-cushion moulded into a corner, her book-wrapper on the grass. The East was like a green pit, long shadows and iridescence and farewells. The sun in the West had sunk. Nurse faced the blown narcissi from last night's gale and thought only of how these girls act and what trouble they make and how she would like to shift the lump onto the squire's shoulders. But the squire has gone in.

The white apron fluttered like the broken narcissi. Up the garden a head of grass rose in a turf-ride to the line of stables. The evening buckets clanked, and the throb of the tap, turned on with its worn washer, stubbled and stuttered down the long pipes. "She'll have to see to that," thought Nurse (thinking of the squire).

Then she remembered the baby. Again and again and again Nurse remembered the baby. Thinking of it at the turns of passages, waking, sleeping, bending, washing, counting linen. Though this was her lady's fifth birth, to Nurse it was yet like being in love, it was the prince arriving; core and stomach of her work; leap and triumph of her virgin maternity. Her soul swelled but gave place to her tabulating mind. Even there in the garden she went over her implements, the list that the midwife had sent her, and her own list that she would need when she "took over."

Tiresome that the squire was such an expert. And, thank God, she would feed her own baby.

7

Theoretically, and too with all her honest heart she believed in breast-feeding, but nooked away somewhere was the down-pushed knowledge that bottle-feeding was more fun—for her. He who feeds the dog is the dog's master. The green pit had gone grey, and Nurse came in, armed and soothed, to face her girl. Time too to bath Henry.

Henry was withdrawn from the squire's bedroom and made naked in his beauty and soaped. He was on the verge of losing his kingdom. Nurse bustled with him abstractedly. When the last one was in bed she would finish the double appliqué on the cot pillow. If only the squire would let her drape the cot! But she would have it airy with the basketwork free from material.

"Lucky I kept that lavender from last summer well-lidded-up. It'll do for his sachets for his basket." She wiped her eye from the squirt of Henry's tin pump. Henry, whose crown was slipping from his silver head, pulled up the plug of the bath and stopped the hole with his heel.

8

"Let that water out now!"

Henry let it out intermittently, examining the fit of his heel through the cloudy water.

"There's three to take baths after you, Henry!"

He glanced at her. She was not cold but withdrawn. His crown was halfway down his back had he known (and he had an inkling).

Nurse pulled out the four-year baby, set him on his feet, rubbed him down, towelled him and sat him by the fire. She left the bathroom and called "Boniface!" through the nursery door.

There came a sharp scream racking and short.

Boniface crouched on the floor with a scarlet face reading the *Commercial Motor*.

"Boniface!"

He screeched again like a parrot, without moving his eyes off the page.

"Nobody'd think you were seven!"

He curdled her blood with his answering yell, hardly moving a muscle, and reading, reading for dear life. Under her quiet gaze he

folded his magazine with a reasonable sigh and
followed her into the bathroom.

"Screaming like an animal! I don't know
where you get the breath to do it!"

He grinned but said nothing and began to
pull off his sweater over his head.

"When I scream," said Henry, rubbing the
fireguard down with his toes and up with his
toe-nails, "you can see me doing it. Boniface
does his in his throat."

"Get on and dry your legs," said Nurse.

"They're dried," said Henry.

"Where's Jay and Lucy?" said Nurse to
Boniface.

He shook his red face, wasting no word.

Out of the bathroom window, across the
Green, behind black swags and bouquets of
ilex, the bedroom window of the other house
flashed on. So sharp, firing light into her
window, that Nurse looked up and looked
down again.

A slim arm pulled the curtains across the
way.

"She's down there," said Nurse.

"That lady?" said Henry.

"Mummie's friend."

(Not the kind of lady, thought Nurse instantly, to bear a newborn baby as it should be born, as the squire would bear it. Not the kind of lady to nurse it afterwards. Not a soldier . . . thought Nurse strangely, her mind running on the barracks where she was born. A sweet lady, lovely like a lily, but not a soldier. What a funny thing to think! But not the kind of mother her kind of nurse went to. Nurse felt pride in her heavy squire, her argumentative, provoking squire.)

"Say 'good evening' to Mrs. Pascoe," nudged Nurse, for there was a presence in the doorway, a shadow across the bath.

Henry lifted his blond lashes and said good evening soberly, with a disciplined reverence to the woman who could make or mar Nurse's supper. Useless to nudge Boniface to say anything.

Mrs. Pascoe, coming down from her rest to staff supper, surveyed the scene without tenderness. But liked Henry's manners.

"Mr. Pratt's been telling me that we're to expect . . . (Nurse looked up sharply) the lady in the case in a day or two."

"That's right. Any day now. She's on call."

"Trays, I suppose. And messages coming down to the kitchen through the housemaids and what not."

Nurse's heart swelled with contemptuous anger, but she restrained it. "Don't worry, Mrs. Pascoe. She's been here before an' no trouble."

Mrs. Pascoe pushed back her red hair from her wiry face. "Yes, before my time. Mr. Pratt's none too keen. Running and scurrying and girls giving notice and something in the air that turns my stomach! I tell you what, Nurse, I can tend a death but I've no nerve for birth!"

"Funny . . ." said Nurse abstractedly, bumping Henry upright onto a chair to clean his teeth.

"Well, it's your job, of course. You couldn't be expected to feel the same. But I don't like being in a house where this is happening."

("She's never going to give notice," thought Nurse. "Just now!")

"I was sending you up a macaroni cheese and a bit of puff-trimmings and Tiptree," said Mrs. Pascoe, preparing to pass on downwards. "If there's anything else?"

"Unless you've got a cold chicken leg," called Nurse, who hated macaroni cheese.

"Done into rissoles," said Mrs. Pascoe shortly, and went on down the stairs.

Nurse let out her breath in an angry gust. Wet macaroni enough to hump up in the chest all night, and the woman going to give notice. Her puff was beautiful. Came up like a concertina, but what a woman! To talk like that about the sacred prince, the lovely baby. Funny how they go queer down there against the stoves.

Nurse resolved to warn the squire of the conversation. That, and her girl, and Mr. Pratt. She would try and catch the squire after dinner.

Pratt bent his tall figure over the library fire, fire-tongs in hand. The library was empty, the squire gone up to dress. Tck! The lights went out. Only the firelight lit his trousers. The lights on that circuit had fused.

The circuit involved the squire's bedroom above, the staircase and the landing outside. He heard her calling for a candle. He stood still (a dignified, black figure, holding the fire-tongs) because his smouldering nature was accustomed to save itself by inaction. Let her mend her fuse. And yet he liked the squire. The hyacinths smelt clear in the dark and the fire warmed his knees.

The squire did not call his name. If she had called that he would have gone. Instead he heard her coming down the stairs, heavy tread and steady descent, and go to her Wellington cabinet in the passage. He heard the candle set upon the wood, the opening of a drawer (screwdriver, fuse-wire), he heard the squire tread out into the hall and the sigh of the baize door closing after her.

You had to keep yourself to yourself, and

let things slide, and never open your eyes too wide, and the days would trundle along. There were bitter moments of gloom. You had to snatch comforts against them. Food, for instance, and inaction, and books. He did not drink. If he had drunk perhaps he could have tolerated the women better. Hateful women! Surrounded by gibbering, preening, untruthful, slovenly women. But he liked the squire. He had no tenderness towards her condition and he would not lift a finger to help her, but he liked her.

They were sitting down to supper in the "Hall" now. He gazed into the fire. Women down two sides of the table (Mrs. Pascoe at the head) waiting for the lights to come on (for the squire had cut the house-current off undoubtedly), giggling in the dark, prodding the kitchen-boy, boasting and laughing. Or sitting silent and pinched like the housemaids, withdrawn, like ailing cats. Tck! The lights came on.

He did not hear the squire's return but saw her framed in the doorway looking at him.

She took it all in, she knew him from head to foot. Lazy brute! But they were not enemies. Without a word she went back and up to her bath.

*   *   *   *

She who had once been thirsty and gay, square-shouldered, fair and military, strutting about life for spoil, was thickened now, vigorous, leonine, occupied with her house, her nursery, her servants, her knot of human lives, antagonistic or loving. Twelve years married to a Bombay merchant and nearly five times a mother, she was well-accustomed to her husband's long absences, and to her own supreme command.

"But to leave you this time through a birth!" he had said. "I have never left you through a birth!"

"It's the one time to leave me," she had replied. "I shall be sunk in stupefied content. The edge will be gone from all my sharp sensations, good or bad. And you will come back and find a two-months' child!"

So he had gone, and took the gaiety of his happy presence with him, his easy command, his shattering of routine, the vigorous and incidental thing he made of daily life. The house emptied of the friends he brought, his own rooms were dusted and folded away, letters came and went across the sea. Lying in the water now, putting her strong hands with the blunt fingers on the bath's lip, with shrewd and watchful eyes the steward whom he had left behind looked upwards through the steam. Invitation had gone now from her face, expectancy had gone, replaced by a lonelier but happy look. "In a strange way," she thought, "these absences suit my nature though not my heart. I love him, I miss him, but I have time to put on my humanity again." She felt gay. If she could have whistled in tune she would have whistled in her bath. She produced a tuneless sound and stopped, from habit—floundering happily in the water, huge and light as a sea lion.

CHAPTER TWO

THE SQUIRE PUT ON HER ANCIENT evening clothes. She looked fine, ruddy and erect, walking heavily, the iron-blue, crumpled drapery hanging from her neck to her feet. Eyes and mouth half-smiling expectantly towards her meal, hair crisp (not a grey hair). Pratt at her order crossed over to the other house, where the garden gate swung and there were wheel-marks on the gravel. "Would her ladyship come over to her ladyship for coffee?"

But the answer was that Lady Caroline had driven away at seven.

So the squire was alone for the evening and Caroline was off again. Some man had whistled on the telephone to her and Caroline had been drawn away. This house over the road that she took each summer for a retreat had no door strong enough to hold her, no balm to give to Caroline, lovely and restless, victim and adventurer. The squire smiled, well satisfied with herself. She was beyond all that, beached like a ship that has been through a gale. Holding the disguising dress about her she trod down to dinner.

There was a cushion for the back of her chair. Pratt pushed the chair in beneath her and adjusted the glass screen between her back and the small fire. She sat, a little grim, and sniffed the food, her eyes gazing between the four flames of the candles, thinking of other things.

"Well, well, well . . ." (aloud, for she was getting to talk alone) as Pratt handed her a dish of braised beef and carrots. He bent a little as though he was to hear a further command; but nothing came.

"I didn't think," said the squire to herself, "I should be so pleased with middle age." Over the great slopes of her own body her eyes dwelt on Caroline, her restless fever. "You *can't* go *on and on!*" said the squire, and asked aloud for the port. Pratt unstoppered the master's decanter without emotion. His lady liked port in her gravy. Now her thoughts were spinning out easily by the yard, keeping her chatty company, thinking of love, and Caroline. She hardly noticed when Pratt had attended to her and left the room. Life was so warm, so easily forgotten. Acts of love resembled one another. Only the approaches were different—the ecstasy of avowals, or of advances made before avowals. But even those were indistinguishable from the perch of this full rich middle life. Or had she forgotten?

She admitted she must have forgotten. Lovers dark and fair had dropped from her like fruit off a tree. She had been female to them then, but now what was left standing at the core was the rock of neutral human stuff, neither male nor female. With this she joined hands with humanity; the mysterious foliage of "woman" had died off the rock. "I don't whine after those dishes!" she thought, almost rubbing her hands with appreciation of her journey.

She rang the bell, finished with her braised
beef. The parlourmaid crept in like a mouse,
for Pratt was putting coal again upon the
drawing-room fire.

At the far end of the rambling house a little
white silk dress with forget-me-nots upon the
shoulders was lying its length upon the
parlourmaid's bed.

"Queenie," said the squire, bringing her
eyes into focus with difficulty, and using the
absurd name which she ought to have altered
when she engaged her, "there's a dance down
in the village to-night. If Pratt says you can go
I do too."

Queenie thanked her neatly. She was
unstabbed by conscience, and had meant to go
anyway. She looked upon her little bedroom
as a temporary rabbit hole. There were a
thousand others in the great warren of employ-
ment into which she could pop. She withdrew
the plate primly, thinking of the kitchenmaid.
Ruby might use the broken pane of glass, but
Queenie now "had permission." Much more
comfortable. And she could openly make

chocolate at two in the morning in the kitchen for both of them. They could drink out of the same cup.

Pratt came through the door. Queenie melted back into the hall to fetch the fruit salad. The four candle-flames guttered as the door closed and the squire slid into a trance of dozing thought.

*   *   *   *

Boniface upstairs could not sleep. He was murmuring big words in the dark, well-applied but mispronounced. In the peace of night his veiled speech cleared, the eager horses of his mind galloped as they should, with beautiful hooves, driven at speed. Lucy heard him. Lying on her side in bed in the room next door she listened to the voice soar and drop and mouth its words, despotically lecturing in the dark. He who could not in the light conclude his sentences, left out his nouns, let go his half-voiced thoughts so that they wandered away, never to be caught again, he, when dark fell, defeated sleep and talked aloud in his room with a droning, steady clarity.

Meanwhile, flinging his body nervously in the bed, he wound and unwound his bedclothes, and even his mattress shifted from the wall, his pillow dropped to the floor, his glass of water was upset.

Lucy saw the line of light snap on and rose on her elbow in bed. But before she could get up the door opened and Boniface came out, stumbling, holding his unfastened pyjama-legs up by the string, his face scarlet, hair on end, crossing the room to the nursery door.

"Boniface!"

But he went on and passed into the day nursery. Lucy held her breath, and lay down again in the dark.

The day nursery was empty, and Boniface went on, making for his mother, going down the stairs on bare feet, one hand on the rail, one holding the dropping pyjamas. "Do up the tape!" said Pratt (like a statue in the hall) but Boniface, filled with his idea, was deaf. He reached the door and went in and saw his mother stare at him across the candles.

"Do up the tape!" she said at once, seeing him nearly naked.

"No waist," said Boniface desperately, walking in a circle. He trod round and round with his lower lip dropping. "No waist." His burning idea was escaping him in this talk of tape. He waved his thin arm, trod round and round, mourned the evaporation of what he came to say. His self-control covered him no thicker than a glaze of cellophane. His mother watched him and knew that with one breath of sympathy he would break.

"Boniface!"

He went round and round, his lips moving, his eyes cast down.

"Boniface! Sit down!" And in a sharp voice: "Have some fruit salad!"

He held up his head and drew a sigh as his trance left him, looking uncertainly at what she offered.

"How dull," she thought, seeing all that the shape of his face meant to her, the unfolding of the seven years of his past, "are the faces of children who are not mine! Dull as the faces

of men who are not one's lovers!" She rang
her bell that Pratt might bring an extra plate.
But Boniface who had sat down pushed it
away when it came and stood up.

"I don't want any," he said with abstracted
sharpness, devoid of offence, and moved off
towards the door, the pyjamas drooping again.

"Good night," said his mother, longing for
him to stay. "Say 'good night'."

"Good night," said he without looking
round, and plunged forward, head lowered, to
rejoin his subterranean plans in the dark pit of
his room.

Sitting, when he had gone, solid like
Queen Victoria on a dais, the squire thought of
her family and her children as an old actress
thinks of the stage. The children drew her,
fatigued, devoured, but drew her. One by one
they rose like apparitions out of the witches'
cauldron and addressed her as though she were
another Macbeth interrogating the future.
"Boniface" . . . What man's name had held
her with such tenderness, such memory of
effort and hope as his? (But this was unfair; she

25

did not now remember the glamour of love.)
Boniface, red of face, asking no help, intent
upon some inner life which would not swim
up into his difficult speech. Boniface, unhelpable, resolved to lead the life of a man before
he was fit to leave babyhood for childhood.
Inarticulate, eccentric, living like a mole in his
world, putting into dangerous execution plans
to which no one had the key. Stitches in his
hand and forehead before he was four, half-
gassed at the gas-ring, half-chloroformed at the
medicine cupboard, and not because he was
mischievous, but because of those projects of
which no one knew beforehand. He was not
daring, not vainglorious, but alone with his
thoughts, oblivious to the height of walls, the
softness of his body, the liquid depths of water.

"If Boniface gets through," thought his
mother. "If Boniface pulls it off!" And she
gasped, sucking in her lip.

Behind Boniface, sheltered, overgrown by
Boniface, came something smaller still, called
by nicknames, endearments, diminutives.
Could it be called Henry, the creature like a

resolute angel that ran naked in the garden in the summer, with dirty feet that picked up leaves with the toes? It was called Henry; and would slowly draw on "Henry" like a cloak, carving its own coffee-coloured face into thought, brushing the silver tufts on its head with oil, wrapping its skin in the uniform of man so that only very privileged women would then see how Henry grew—from his feet to his knees, from his knees up his dappled and quilted legs, from his flat stomach to his swelling ribs, and over the shining shoulder to the face of Henry adulterated with life. Henry grown wise. Henry reflecting.

The creature that ran now in the garden in summer was no more wise than kind. It was filled with desire from top to toe. It reached, stretched, felt, pulled, stole and demanded. And all the time that it desired and demanded and play-acted and was filled with a wild lust for possession it went cloaked in beauty, with a face and body of silk and satin.

This did not melt the squire, nor the brothers and sister, nor his nurse. They had had ten

years of babies, some of them. They knew that
this divine thing could slip its glory and
become a nursery menace, and the sister and
brothers watched with lynx eyes for signs of
weakness in the elders. When Henry desired
and was refused, then his brow reddened, his
face grew scarlet, and he flung himself backwards upon the ground, shooting his bolt.
Then Lucy, the sister, would tweak her brother
Jay's sleeve, whispering. "Come away. Don't
look at him. He's showing off!" And Henry,
watching them with his wild thrush's eye, and
seeing their cold receding backs, would know
his bolt was shot; and, having failed, he dismissed his desire.

He matched his strength with theirs all day
long. All day long he watched for openings,
watched for matches, drawing-pins, scissors,
butter, jugs of milk, substances, qualities,
things that would crash, would tip, would pour,
would squelch, would glitter. He put his
finger into holes. Into the cane holes of the
chair-seat, into empty knots in the wood floor,
into channels where they stuck and would not

come out. It was as though his thought not
perfectly and constantly clarified into speech
his mind flickered restlessly in his fingers.
Like the blind and the dumb his hands spoke
for him. His eyes saw and his hands asked.
His own toys he threw away like a lesson
learnt.

He knew certain obediences. Not obedience
to the unexpected, but obedience to the yoke
of his routine. When he was laid down at
night he never murmured, hardly troubled to
watch the receding back. Food he ate. And if
he refused it was not caprice but his beautifully
ordered stomach which dictated his refusal.
His delicate instincts, like those of a wild
animal, though they were still his mentors,
were dying away under the puzzled and rising
voices of man.

Boniface, the lately-ousted, the last king to
get from his throne, had strange thoughts
about him. The squire could see, by murmurs
and tangents, that Boniface had this in mind.
So it was that each child in turn had watched
the lap-enveloped baby, the bathing, the

nursing, and with that queer inability to savour the present had felt the yearning for yesterday's evaporating past.

Thinking of them, sitting in dazzled silence, a little drugged, a little mystic, thoughts and pictures drifted slowly to the edge of the mother's mind, hung and returned, so slender was the breeze of impetus.

And from them all at last her eyes were lowered, the eyes of her mind lowered their lids, and she glanced with them at the embryo, impersonal, saying nothing to her, the companion. She had no tenderness for it, only the keenest expectation. It had no youth, it was old, filled with instinct. It acted like a god, as her master, directing her. She had no control over it. It had nothing to do with the born baby that was to fall with a crash from age to trembling youth, that, once born, would throw up its mastery and lie, shocked and naked, just within the gates of the world.

But now, at the table, behind the fall of the tablecloth, behind the sheath of skin, hanging head downwards between cliffs of bone, was

the baby, its arms all but clasped about its
neck, its face aslant upon its arms, hair painted
upon its skull, closed, secret eyes, a diver
poised in albumen, ancient and epic, shot with
delicate spasms, as old as a Pharaoh in its tomb.

* * * *

Though there was so little to do Pratt spun
that little out, half-atrophied in movement, his
smouldering rage forming ashes upon his mind.

"Why let the creature go to the dance
because the creature must needs ask?"

His blunted hands, so ill-suited to his indoor
body, rinsed a wineglass under the pantry tap.
Slowly he laid a tray for the morning's breakfast and set it on a shelf, slowly gathered the
coffee things together and walked off towards
the dining-room with the tray.

She hadn't come out yet, (thinking of his
lady); there was still light under the dining-
room door. What was she doing dozing in
there and he not able to get at her fruit plate
to wash it and set it away? His skin was
growling, like the hair of an old dog.

She hadn't got to wash the fruit plate when she let Queenie off; easy for her to say yes to things that creatures asked. He stood back, holding the tray as the dining-room door opened and the squire came out. His small eyes glanced down his cheeks upon the tray, eyes with a mixture of meanness and fire, his back a little arched against the weight he held, holding the silver handle at each end.

"Queenie gone?" said the squire affably. A murmur came from his lips, low, sullen, disciplined, antagonistic. And she, looking up at the face which confirmed the murmur, moved on ahead of him, snatched uncomfortably out of her dream.

"Curse him!" she thought irritably, but gave him no opening. As he offered the tray and she took first the silver coffee-pot and then the jug of boiling milk the cages of their angry breasts stood up like enemy fortresses.

"Pratt," she said aloud (to shake him by her news out of his brooding, to give him something to grumble at if he wanted it), "to-morrow my midwife comes."

It was true he was pulled up out of his dark storm, astonished. Was the baby as near as that. Years he had been with her, but he could never quite get over her sudden and calm deliveries.

"Her room, I know, is ready. I've seen to that. But you'll see that her breakfast trays go up as they should do? I know you will, but you must watch Queenie."

He concurred gravely. As one who should know the ignorance and the sauce of Queenies.

"And Mrs. Pascoe . . ." dwelt the squire doubtfully, wondering if she could fish a little security from him, "Mrs. Pascoe? Do you think she means to see me through this in peace?" (The squire, without Nurse's help, had her ear to the ground.)

Pratt took a line he seldom took. He never interfered, he never registered a coming storm. He liked to let it break, rocking the tough squire, and himself retiring to the pantry say, "Let her see what we put up with!" But now he knew he was to be without his squire, the reins to lie idle for a fortnight and Mrs. Pascoe to wreck his peace with her ginger-headed virginity, her malicious prudish anger at the birth. So forcing himself he went so far as to say that Mrs. Pascoe was unsettled.

"Unsettled, is she!" snorted the squire with hot rage, "I should like to unsettle her!"

"It might be wise," she heard Pratt answer and she paid instant, sharp attention, "to ask Mrs. Pascoe if she would not prefer to leave before."

"Before the baby comes! At once!"

"It might be wise to ask her," said Pratt.

The squire's hands began to tremble, her heart under her breast grew uneven, the sudden passions her condition rendered her liable to coming hot in her.

"I'll see her at once."

He looked at his large watch. "It's nine o'clock," he said. "She may have gone to her room. Perhaps it might be better in the morning?"

"I can't sleep with this hanging over me!" said the squire. "The baby might start any moment, and nothing settled. But you don't

mean she'd go at once, to-morrow? Is that
what she wants?"

"It's what she says," said Pratt. "But in the
kitchen they don't mean half they say."

"Send her in!" said the squire, and walked,
flaming, about the room, the blood risen in
her face.

Mrs. Pascoe did not come at once. She had
not gone to her room, but stood trifling in her
kitchen, that the squire might have time to regret
this most unusual message that Pratt had brought
her. Meanwhile despair, anger, indignation engulfed the squire. "At the very last ditch!" she
muttered. She was in no mood to regret her
message. Her heart beat angrily in her tightly
packed body. There was already, before it began, no hope of this interview going off well.

At length the door opened and the cook
entered, paused under the doorway and stood
with all her mysterious reserves.

The flowers in the vases seemed to listen.

"I wanted to tell you, Mrs. Pascoe, that the
trained nurse who is to look after me arrives
to-morrow."

Mrs. Pascoe remained without movement. The statement did not explain why she had been sent for at this hour.

"I wanted to make sure," said the squire steadily, "that you knew that the baby might be born any time now. I have told Pratt and I am telling you (for after all it may even be to-night), and I hope you will do your best to keep things running smoothly for me."

"I shall do my duty," said Mrs. Pascoe, in a voice empty of every human decency.

"I hope you will do even more!" said the squire sharply. "Babies aren't born every day."

"I should like you to take my notice," said Mrs. Pascoe instantly, as though she had found what she had been looking for.

"Why?" said the squire, very loud and short.

"I should like a change," said Mrs. Pascoe, trumping that trick.

"It comes to this . . ." said the squire, her heart throbbing again, "If I don't hurry up and have this baby, your month may be up before I am out of bed!"

Mrs. Pascoe made no answer.

"Ah . . ." muttered the squire thickly, walking to her writing-desk while the woman in the doorway waited.

"You can dam' well go to-morrow!" said the squire in another rage, with gusto putting herself in the wrong. (A month's wages, a month's board, insurance, washing money, it was worth it to get rid of this woman who didn't care whether she had her baby in peace or not.)

"I shall be glad," said Mrs. Pascoe drily, "to be away before the event."

"I'll bet you will!" said the squire, and the door shut.

So in a dozen words of wrath the reign and the power of Mrs. Pascoe was broken. The squire went round her children, putting out the lights as she went. Far away, down by the sea, Ruby and Queenie danced. And far away in a room at the north end of the house Mrs. Pascoe with twitching hands, pulled off her clothes.

The lights from a car coming up from the

sea swept like a searchlight over the ceiling of
Henry's room where he lay, sleeping, turned
towards the door, his lashes in arcs of olive
shadow on his cheek. His mother, her heart
still thumping, stooped with a grunt and kissed
him.

Then on to Boniface's room, his battlefield.
Asleep now, he had fought with his blankets
as though they were his ideas. His mother
dragged his limp body, limp and heavy as a
ship's cable, back into the centre of his bed
and folded him securely like a parcel. His
sleep was the heavy sleep of exhaustion and
spent effort.

As she stood over him she knew that she
no longer said to herself "My life, my future"
. . . but "their lives, their future . . ." Now,
well past forty she was beginning to pack her
box. (And she tried hard to hope that there
would be a journey.)

"When you have given birth," she thought,
going into Lucy's room, "when too you have
lost your mother, then indeed you begin to
look about you with suspicion, to smell, so

faintly, what it is to die! I cannot prevent myself beginning to live for others."

As she stood by Lucy's bed she thought of Mrs. Pascoe with dismay. Was it possible to understand another creature so little? What would she find if her spirit crept now into bed by Mrs. Pascoe's spirit and lay probing it, looking it in the eye in the dark? Would Mrs. Pascoe's spirit live and die, and fly through space for ever like a rocket of hate? The reign and the power of Mrs. Pascoe was broken, but the squire was left aching as though she had had a blow. That she had put herself in the wrong by her temper was also annoying. And the complicated cheque to be written . . . Phew! She looked down at Lucy and then up again at the moon.

Where the moon shone over the lovely churchyard lay her mother whom passionately the squire had loved. Her mother, who, unaware, had taught to her child all the anticipations of death. Trembling, irritable, aching with apprehension she had watched her mother spend herself upon life. Since she was nine years old the squire had waited for only one parting, had said to herself "It will come like this—it will be like that!" Often in the night she had woken and divined in a flash all the desolation of loss. But as she grew older she had learnt to govern and disperse these visitations of dread.

Now in her own little girl she encountered the same irritable and aching eye.

But whatever else was spoken of between the squire and Lucy this at least was a subject about which to be quiet. If by luck the dread flower was not yet planted she, the mother, must not blow one seed upon the wind. This little girl on the bed, she liked to put out roots. As some trees are, she was tough-rooted. When her roots were drawn from her earth by superior force she wept. Even when the earth was poor and hard she rooted again and was content. So long as one day followed another and she could get a hold on its flow she was content. To be shifted from one place to another, to be shifted from one habit to another, to be shifted along the years (even by the silver pressure of a birthday) this was something she fought against with every weapon in her constant heart.

The boys lived like gay lambs in a field. They did not muse but looked forward in hourly expectation to the next pleasure. Even Boniface thought nothing of himself, or of his position in life in respect to his surroundings. It was this child, Lucy, who seemed to have been born with the strong impression of the axe. "Axed—my babyhood! Axed—my baby privileges! Axed—those white dresses, so short, that I wore last summer! (Something is gone with their going.) Axed—the whole long summer and one set of flowers after another! Axed—the love of dolls, and fiddling with the dolls' house." One thing after another had melted away. The regretting eyes could not fix themselves upon the future. Deep below the child's mind stewed the vapour which would rise when the time was ready. "Axed—my mother. Axed—my life."

"Some are born stricken with knowledge,"

thought the squire, as she watched the moon. "Some are free."

She passed from Lucy to Jay. The walls seemed transparent as she slipped through them, her expectation of each face printed behind her eyes. As she laid her hand on each door-knob the face of the child within shone upon the panel, and as the door opened the child itself, whether asleep on the bed or springing like a jack-in-the-box to greet her, replaced the Precursor. The children seemed to cast their Precursors like shadows about the house, sometimes tangibly, in the sound of a voice, sometimes by suggestion, because it was striking the hour for their return from a walk, sometimes mysteriously, because inside the shell of their mother's head the children were painted like angels on the roof of a chapel.

Angels the squire thought them. Now worn wise by life herself she could not remember that she too had perhaps been born a little wise. She was continually aware that the qualities the children showed were none of her direct implanting. Intuition, tact, occasional odd and uncertain sophistications, good-feeling, sudden reticences, kindnesses, these grew among them like flowers whose roots had sown themselves, and the squire was again and again aware that these were the young of God's major animal. Tenderly and angrily she thought of them, and of herself too, as too good for death.

Jay had his sheet over his head like a cowl. When she uncovered him she saw that he was pink and wet with sweat. But no longer was she thinking of the children. Raising her eyes to that moon which had sailed further along and was in the corner of the window it struck her with foolish optimism that now she would get the perfect cook. Now, free of Mrs. Pascoe, she would get that soft and bonny woman, loving to children, ready with the iced cakes on Sundays, ready to do the old-fashioned things that should be done with fruit, quince-bottling, crab-apple-jellying: basins of home-made shrimp paste on Saturdays, pounded chickens' livers, dripping saved for the nursery. A cook, ample and kind, more like an old nurse than a cook. She would write to the registry offices before she went to bed. Jay, who looked like Henry grown bigger but no older, gave an uncertain smile in his sleep and threw himself on his back. The squire docked the moon from his face with the tip of a curtain tucked tautly under the mattress, then, not daring to kiss him, she left him. He came up through his sleep, his eyes opened, and closed again.

Back in the garden-room she wrote letters till midnight. To the registry offices what she wrote was drier than the burning hope behind the pen. At midnight when the fire had burnt down, and leaving the door wide open that she might have the lights behind her, she went through the dark hall, drew back the bolts of the front door and took her letters to the post.

The village green outside was white with moonlight. As she stepped on to it it seemed a deck, her village ship a-sail on the slant of the world. The unknown and impersonal companion within her turned with a gulp, emitted a bubble of wind and revolved in its pond.

44

"Do you never sleep?" she enquired aloud of her belly. The hemispheres whirled above the stillness, stars shone; down at human level the lamp in the churchyard gate was still as a star.

After forty the sense of beauty grows less acute; one is troubled instead by a vast organ note, a hum of death. Not so the squire. Drifting towards the birth of her baby with a simple and enchanted excitement she walked in radiance like a bride.

Coming back from post, roving like a house-dog about her house, glancing up at the windows where the children slept, every bush, every white corner of the house moved her as she placed her hand on the garden gates to see that they were locked. A faint smell of horses was drifting on the night air, touched with manure and seaweed. The cold ivy on an archway rustled. Walking in the dark, swelling so full of life, she felt, in the bravado of birth, that she knew what was the matter with life. "Death is the matter with life," she said. "That this should end!"

*   *   *   *

45

At two, while the squire dozed in bed, the soft sea-mist came crowding against the door and windows. It chilled the rooks and while the squire rootled in her bed and tried to shut it out, one, colder than the rest, complained in the tree above the house. The sea-mist sank down through the air and hung in a thin spread on the warmth of the earth, and melted. The rook was quiet but the squire turned slowly that she might not strain her stretched muscles, and sitting up she put on the light and began to read. But even so the child seemed to have risen into her throat, and supporting the inhabited stomach with both her hands she got out of bed and walked barefoot in the corridor. Nothing was altered in the night as yet. She went through the three doors into the day-nursery and leant out of the window to the summer street, dewy and damp before dawn. Caroline's house was dark behind the ilex branches. Far away a car was coming along the sea road. Its beam struck the opposite hill, turned where the street turned up the valley, came up between the line of cottages to the Green, and blazed upon the whiteness of the cobbled walls. Then the hand on the wheel dimmed the headlights and the car floated nearer, its interior lit like a golden cage. Leaning with a rush of interest from the window the squire saw the white shirt-front of a man beside her friend. (Caroline, driving back from the opera in London.) The car stood still under the wall, a yellow box of glamour, and the village, the night, the shadowed ilexes, but not the squire's heart, were illumined by it.

"It's all definitely over," thought the squire of herself. "I can take nothing of that sort any more."

And when the two had gone through the gate and the car had stolen round to the garage the squire leant against the window, neither hot nor cold.

"But I can do without it," she said. (The baby moved.) "Love should be over sooner than it is. We catch fish and throw nets too long, and the fish themselves get smaller and smaller inside the net. We deck ourselves too long!"

The lights in Caroline's bedroom went on, soft, behind the curtains. The squire dropped her eyes from the light, not from modesty or envy, but because she wanted the unborn to sleep undisturbed. The dew-wet road crossed the grass on the empty Green. Box beside box stood the little houses down the street to the sea, hedges about the gardens coated with darkness.

It was just before dawn. Birds' eyes blinked in the hedges, hooded and unhooded. Now a gold orb—click—and shut again like a camera. And inside the cottages in the street the babies were waking—gayer eyes, less wild, fresh as daisies.

The watcher leant steadily on the window-sill and reckoned up in her mind the inhabitants, saw them through the walls where they lay, neatly like the dead, mothers, nurses, maids, cooks, gardeners, carpenters, cobblers— heavily as the dawn neared, racked with dreams, or empty.

Turning she went back to her room and lay down, rolling onto her side. With the onslaught of extreme fatigue she fell suddenly asleep.

Down the village street the babies went on waking, trying on their tricks in the dark. Some stood on their heads and feet so that they split their wrappings far apart; some drummed with their feet on the bed and worked the wool off the blanket between their toes. The very young let their arms lie fallow and hammered with their feet. All had their thrush's eyes fixed on the humped bed whence would come the divinity of companionship.

The gold orbs in the hedges blinked more rapidly. A bird's cry pierced the silence. There was a pause. Then like cymbals came the reply. All the birds in the hedges burst into voice. The black veils cleared slowly off the gardens. The trees swam into light, bone dry. The day began white, before the sun rose.

CHAPTER THREE

THE CHILDREN'S BACON WAS FRIZZLING and the smell poured round the walls from the kitchen. The squire sniffed and woke. Birds alighting on the gutter scuffled like mice, and beneath her window, barely louder, went the soft noise of shoeless feet.

Upon the lawn lay a football left over from the evening's play, and further, by the frog-pond, where a broken branch hung down, a handkerchief full of pebbles which had been tied to the branch yesterday now dragged the branch lower so that the handkerchief was painted with the green froth from the pond.

Boniface in his vest crossed the lawn to the frog-pond, carrying a bucket.

"After frog-spawn," thought the squire leaning out. "But all the frog-spawn's gone!"

At the edge of the pond he struggled with his

vest and got it off, then waded in the green scum of the water, stooped, and dredged with his bucket.

He should have been sitting in at breakfast. Through the partitions of wood and brick the squire imagined the early scurry in the nursery, Nurse's voice raised, Boniface missing. She heard other, slippered, feet.

"Lucy!" (leaning out of the window).

Lucy looked up at her mother.

"Couldn't you wipe him up and get him back again?" (hanging as best she could over the hard window-ledge).

"I bin sent to look for him," said Lucy.

"Wait!" The squire got out of bed, fetched a towel, threw it to her. "Wipe him with that, and get him back."

The naked child in the pond looked round as Lucy neared him, then stooped to the water. The squire knew what look was in his eyes— not of refusal, not of obstinacy, but of absolute absorption. He felt on the floor of the pond with his hands.

"He's dropped something," she thought,

and remembered the search yesterday for Boniface's cog-wheels tied with string that he called his watch.

She sunk her head on her hands and gazed— stooped over the stretched walls which housed her mysterious child.

Lucy, in striped cotton, ready for breakfast, stood on the edge of the pond and commanded. The green scum rose up Boniface's legs. Lucy held out the towel, offering promises, wanting to save the glory of his morning intact, defend him against his idiotic persistence, keep him from coming trouble. Lucy, though she often hectored him herself, thought Boniface touching and divine. The oncoming of Henry she watched with jealousy and scorn—scorn for those grown people who thought any baby sweeter than any child.

Slowly Boniface came up the bank, green from his waist to his feet, was wiped, his vest drawn on, and with his sister set back across the lawn. Lucy looked up at the squire's window but the squire had gone.

As Lucy and Boniface crossed the courtyard

a gay face hung out of another window, flushed, and with the hard spirits of a boy.

"There they are! There they are!" it cried in excitement and turned to someone within.

"Be quiet, Jay!" hissed Lucy, running up the stairs to him. "Be quiet! Stop it! You'll get him into trouble!"

"Here they are! Here they are!" Jay jumped up and down like a demon. There was a scuffle and Lucy bent and bit him on the shoulder.

Jay turned with his hands clenched, his blue eyes dark. Sobbing, full of pride and pain, choking with anger, black with contempt, hurt to the heart by the suddenness of the attack, baffled, hoping God would strike Lucy dead, he went away to his room. Lucy stood still with horror.

Boniface toiled after her up the stairs, bucket in hand. "It was for *you* I did it!" said Lucy, cold with distress. "I've spoilt the day." She knew she had sprung on the dragon that threatened her young. But the poor dragon, when hit, was soft as an egg-shell.

Standing still, her heart pounding, empty of

anger—"Nurse will know!" she thought. "Bitten him! Are my teeth poisonous?"

Jay was her love and her anxiety now, Boniface was a nuisance. She pushed him into the bathroom.

"Dress yourself," she said roughly. "Your clothes are on the chair."

She tipped his clothes from the chair to the floor in front of him, and dragged the chair beneath the high medicine cupboard fastened to the wall.

"All the morning spoilt . . ." as she looked for the iodine. (Discovery, justice, punishment, reconciliation, all the morning's plans scattered. Was Jay crying?)

Iodine in her hand she pushed open Jay's door.

"I'm sorry, Jay."

Jay turned his rose face, swollen and flushed with tears and anger, towards her. He saw the bottle of iodine and glowered.

"Jay, if I don't . . . people's teeth are dirty."

He put his hand up to the button of his shirt

and let the shirt fall down around his waist.

There were three marks of teeth. Nothing could efface them. Nurse would see at bath time.

"Careful!" said Jay on a high, hysterical note as she unstoppered the bottle. "Quick, then! Wait a minute, wait a minute!" He was upset, flicked his elbow backwards, and the iodine shot out of Lucy's hand in a brown stream over the coverlet of the bed.

Now Lucy, unable to hope any longer, assailed by bad luck, bad acts, and good acts gone wrong, time against her, her teethmarks undeniable, could hold the tottering edifice of control together no longer, and leant against the chest of drawers and wept. Wept, howled, let out a stream of noise and misery, while Jay, pushing her, cried,

"Get to Mummie, get to Mummie! I don't mind the bite!"

Across the courtyard ran Lucy, pounding up the stairway; sobbing she flung herself upon the door of the little room in which the squire was dressing.

Nurse was in there, holding Henry. Henry had a drawing-pin in his toe.

"Got the chocolate?" said the squire.

"Ready," said Nurse.

The squire jerked the drawing-pin free, Henry went back over Nurse's arm in an arc screaming, so that his scarlet face hung upside down, and Nurse deftly stopped his mouth with a piece of milk chocolate. A choking cry and Henry, the pain waning, and the pleasure waxing, came upright again and silently kicked while the squire sucked his toe.

"That was one of your drawing-pins," said the squire to Lucy crossly, and stared at the sight of her face.

"I've spilt the iodine on Jay's bed-cover! I've hurt Jay, I've bitten Jay!"

"Take him back, Nurse," said the squire. "Get on with breakfast. I'll see to Lucy."

Nurse went, with a look at Lucy, taking Henry.

"I'll *never* get dressed!" said the squire, irritated. "What happened?"

The story was told with sobs as the squire did her hair.

"The coverlet's cotton," she said briefly, her mind on the registry offices. "Iodine washes out in cold water. Get on now to breakfast!"

"Can't I have breakfast with you?"

"Blasted cooks," murmured the squire, her head buzzing.

"Can't I have breakfast with you?"

"No, no, NO."

"Why not?"

"No, I say."

"Why not?"

"Don't insist so, Lucy! You've got off cheap. Go and have breakfast and fun and everything. I've got an awful morning before me."

"Why awful?"

"I'm sending Mrs. Pascoe away in an hour. There's no one to cook the lunch."

"Mrs. Pascoe away? Mrs. Pascoe away? For good?"

"Yes, she . . ."

"Nurse *will* be pleased!"

"Why?"

"Nurse hates her. She gives her lumpy suppers. She's always sniffing about the new baby."

"That's why. I may have the baby any day now and Mrs. Pascoe will upset everyone the moment it arrives."

"May you? Any day? To-night?"

"I might," said the squire, looking distractedly for her telephone numbers which were scribbled on a list.

"I got so tired waiting I'd forgotten it could be near," said Lucy slowly, staring at her mother. "It's like a miracle of God."

"It is," said the squire. "It happens every day, to people and animals. But it's a miracle."

"Aren't you afraid?"

"No," said the squire. "No, not a bit. I'm excited."

"I am too," said Lucy and went to her breakfast.

*   *   *   *

Pratt found the window-cleaner prowling in

the garage yard, his light ladder on his
shoulder

"Good morning," said the little man, his
cigarette behind his ear.

Pratt's low voice murmured something
unfathomable and surly. Mrs. Pascoe, depart-
ing, had poisoned the air in the "hall." His
parlourmaid, Queenie, was all yawns, with
flashes of cheek. He was wondering what life
held for him when he saw the little man and
his ladder.

"Lovely . . ." said the window-cleaner,
with a brief look at the flowing air around him.

"Is this your day?"

"Main windows, best spare, an' nurseries."

"Get on then."

"Which'll I do first?"

"Please yourself."

The little man took no offence and whistled
off through the gate.

"For the love of God . . ." thought Pratt,
obscurely disgusted by the fellow's freedom
and pleasure in the day.

The window-cleaner saw the squire in the

courtyard pinning up the honeysuckle. "Near her time," he thought, and his gregarious instincts led him to place his pail beside her. She nodded to him and went inside through the french windows to the telephone. The window-cleaner stepped lightly on his rubber-clad feet, and put his pail on an old piece of sacking. He liked to hear voices while he worked; it made a change to hear someone on the telephone. Deft and unconscientious he rubbed the little panes lightly and quickly, with a circular motion, leaving the square corners untouched, while his thoughts hopped like birds. He opened one of the top windows that he might hear the lady better, and took a puff from his cigarette. A gay, free little man with no manners.

The children came running down through the courtyard. One of them seized a rung of his ladder.

"Stow it," he said, looking down. The child went.

"Cook?" said the lady's voice. She had got through. The morning was so still he could hear the clerk's ghostly reply.

"Temporary or permanent?"

"Temporary."

"Town or country?"

"Country."

"How many in the kitchen?"

"Two."

"How many in the staff?"

"Seven."

"How many in family?"

"Six."

"Name and address," went on the thin voice. The lady gave it, at length, with care and clarity.

"We have no one on our books," the voice said and the conversation shut down.

"Oh!" said the lady, leaning back and putting down the telephone. She looked up and saw him with his circular flying hand, like a shadow.

"You're leaving the corners," she said.

"Coming back to them, Ma'am."

Watching him, she tried another number, and got through.

"Cooks?" said her voice.

"Temporary or permanent?"

"Temporary."

"Hold the line."

"What?"

"The clerk in charge is talking on another line."

"You don't know of a cook, do you?" asked the lady, clinging to the ebonite holder, and leaning on the sofa arm.

"Eh?" said the little man. He had been absorbed in listening.

"A cook. You don't know of a cook?"

He put his rubber politely on his shoulder and poked his head through a top window looking down at her.

"No," he said.

"Don't you ever hear of maids?"

"No," he said again. And then, "I was in service once."

"What were you?"

"Kitchen boy."

"Why can't one get anybody?" said the lady querulously.

"Well," said the little man, "they like their freedom. They're like me; they like getting off at five."

"Cooks!" came the voice of the clerk.

"Hullo, hullo . . ." stammered the lady, getting adjusted, and talked at length, and hung up.

"I hope you were successful, Ma'am," said the window-cleaner, bringing his pail inside.

"Pretty well," said the squire, moving about the room, preoccupied.

She found him agreeable but not interesting —more like a burglar than a window-cleaner, with his deft, irresponsible fingers, and padding, rubbery feet. A brief, half-baked Exister, kept going by something moderate that happened "after five."

But life, she thought, is a series of these moderate anticipations, taking one by the hand and leading one with a hopeful face. Life was immense, so arching, such echoes in it, that to do little acts, to tread along to pleasures not too far ahead, anticipated with gentle excitement, was what carried one on, wound safe as cotton upon a reel.

Outside the window the children swam by in the courtyard like fishes in a pond; up and down, on errands, on searches, voices calling, feet running, faces passing the glass.

Half the morning gone in telephoning! And the temporaries coming at twelve!

The squire looked longingly at her bit of sewing. She sewed stiffly and patiently like a sailor, pushing her needle through with her thumb and pulling it slowly out, watching the floating thread; sewing only when she was with child, sewing as a sedative. Now to save a little peace out of the morning she took a cushion with her, and her sewing to the pond. The day was standing wide open now, ready for action. Right and left the village was at work over the park wall. Smoke trickled up from the cottages; the gully of the village street was filled with heat as with a substance. Lucy came over the lawn—"I'll sit with you," she said.

"Yes, I'll sit with you," said Lucy again. She had been weighing the pleasures in the village against the pleasures of talking to her mother.

"You can sit for a bit," said the squire.

They arranged their cushions on the lawn, but the squire was uncomfortable.

"It'll have to be a chair, Lucy."

The child dragged a canvas chair from the tool-shed.

"Does it hurt having a baby?" she asked.

"No," said the squire alertly. "Not more than a stomach-ache."

The sewing was unrolled. The squire on her lapless lap laid out the tools for work. Scissors, the big needle, the cotton. It was a cretonne coat for Lucy that had accompanied her through the long months now behind her.

"That coat," said Lucy contentedly, "won't be done till the baby's come."

"No," said the squire. "No, I shouldn't think so."

There was silence. While her mother hung suspended in a half-dream the child sat at her feet with the watchful stillness of a terrier. She, the child, felt the hour of the mid-morning calm like something alive. She noted the upright hedges, thick and firm, the light dwelling on the red roofs and bounding off the whitewash on the walls.

"Funny how you can't sew," said Lucy reflectively.

"Look," she said in a minute, her eyes on the pond, "the frogs are out sunning! Let's sit nearer."

They went together to the pond. The frogs, frozen by the movement, sat still. Fourteen golden eyes like nuggets gleamed unwinking from the margin. Some squatted on dead reeds and immersed branches. Tranced by the half-apprehended movement above them they relied for safety upon immobility. Some hung by one slim hand like children to a raft. All had been stricken to stone by the human appearance. Only the sun, shifting in the sky, tickled the fire in the nuggets in their green heads.

"I don't know how Boniface *could!*" said Lucy.

"What?"

"Stick his feet in among all those."

"What was he after? The spawn's gone. Was he after his watch?"

"I don't know," said Lucy. "He was awake before five, and talking to himself."

"He tells us nothing," said the squire, putting down her sewing. "He never asks me anything!"

Suddenly she knew that she would not live for ever to protect him: she would not live for ever. Not one of the frogs knew that. They understood fear and pain, capture, and the panic of escape. Not death. Not old age, not sickness, not death. Not the knowledge of the ultimate morning and the ultimate night. That was reserved for her.

"God's major animal . . ." she said once again—and house, lawns, children sank like an armada in a quicksand. She saw herself alone, alive and doomed, strong and helpless, passing in a line of women, her mother before her, the child Lucy, behind, women walking on a temple frieze, Greek women in fluttering robes rounding a vase's girth for ever.

Lucy moved and the squire's mind thickened. The landscape came back upon the glass.

"Let's," said Lucy, for she had thought of it in the silence, "go down the village and buy doughnuts."

Instantly in the sturdy and responsive mechanism of her mother the digestive juices began to flow. She stepped lightly from her mind into her body, looking at Lucy, the child grinning with delight. On the square face of the mother and in her blue eyes came a look of irony and gaiety. Neither her imagination nor her stomach had ever grown up. Only her wisdom grew older and older.

"All down the village!" she protested. "At eleven?"

"And we could see the sea," said Lucy.

So through the side gate of the garden and out into the yellow village street they strolled, buying doughnuts at the post office and eating them down to the sea.

CHAPTER FOUR

BY TWELVE O'CLOCK THE SQUIRE WAS back, mooning about at midday, waiting for the temporaries. White midday. She ordered a glass of sherry.

Pratt had two glasses of sherry. They gave him some consoling vision. He did not allow himself much, knowing what happened to butlers who drank. His father had been a butler before him. He had been brought up in the old régime, that "good service" his father had talked of in his old age. He had known in his childhood the primness, the narrow, religious life, the sense of duty, the love of order of good head-housemaids, the tyrannical and successful discipline of good cooks, the unwilling, slow, but inevitable bending to duty of "unders." He was a link with an old order, now embittered by the material he found around him, a

trained engineer supplied with tools of tin;
using them as he could for there were no other
tools. But all the beauty of his training was
window-dressing. He could get no real work
out of his subordinates and he would not
betray his order and his accomplishments by
doing himself what should have been the work
of his tools. So, brooding, he surveyed his
loneliness and frustration and found a sort of
company in the squire's quiet knowledge of
him, pitted with angry encounters though
their friendship was.

Drink, no, he would not drink. For two
years, as first-footman in a situation in London,
he had belonged to one of those west-end clubs
where stately men in soft hats, silk scarves and
indoor shoes come silently to a side door when
the day's work is done. Men like Raeburn
pictures, impassive English faces, long-jawed,
faces like actors and bishops, set mouths and
well-groomed heads; there behind a quiet
door some could drink a bottle and a quarter
in an evening. Always whisky; a bottle and
a quarter of whisky; whisky drinkers; able

miraculously to return on duty at eight next morning, steady-headed, foul-tempered and ritualistic. He had known these men, seen how they held out to the last lap, and what was their collapse. How they dropped, ruined, through the rings of service, each ring holding them awhile, till down they went to that hell of penniless men who have been indoor servants and cannot do a hand's turn at a manual job.

Gone like a ship's crew to hell they were. No, he who had the keys of the cellar would never drink. But sometimes life was too black. Couldn't be borne. He took another glass of light sherry and carefully wiped his lips.

There was the squire in there interviewing the temporaries. Venomous adders of temporaries. There were two more that he had just let in, sitting now in the hall. Before God his life was a black one, he thought, carefully hanging his coat on the hook on the pantry door. He had learnt his beautiful trade for nothing. It was the end of service, the outside last limit. These strange, modern creatures

71

were edging away from everything he
understood. The garden light streamed in at
the pantry window, and Pratt felt all the
savagery of the man who is nearing sixty and
has always been on the wrong lines.

In his position he was like a eunuch, he
thought bitterly, his hatred and contempt for
women had sapped his sex; but looking the
spring in the face out of the white morning
window he was lifted and soothed by the last
little glass of sherry. A frond of jasmine waved
above the sill, and having hauled his bitterness
to light he felt as a man who has eased his
stomach and is convalescent.

In the long, low morning-room the squire
sat facing the enemy, one by one.

"As you see," she said, "I am going to have
a baby immediately."

They saw. It had been their instantaneous
preoccupation when they entered the room,
but as temporaries that hardly mattered to
them. They went from situation to situation
with slovenly adaptability, shedding disruption
about the house, Pied Piper whistling to its

rats, a come-up-and-follow-me which got into the blood of the "unders," slackening discipline; playing a take-it-easy tune with the tolerant, bland eyes of old soldiers, untying loyalties, unloosing rules, getting down late, getting in late, and sneaking the miserable perquisites of their calling.

"Mrs. Dummett," ushered Queenie to the squire from the door.

There could never be anything between Mrs. Dummett and the squire. They looked at each other, the one with astonished horror, the other, over the pale trunk of an immense goitre, out of needle-black eyes. Everything that Mrs. Dummett had seen so far, the shape of the house, the shape of the squire, had strengthened her determination to refuse the situation—a situation that she would certainly never be offered. What kind of niche, thought the squire, could Mrs. Dummett fill? What household could adopt into its bosom this woman with malevolent eye? A born lavatory attendant if ever there was one, cloth in one hand, penny in the other. They murmured to

each other with a glancing sharpness, and soon
the squire was fumbling for the return-bus-
fare from an envelope of small coin beside her.

"Mrs. Lynch," said Queenie.

Mrs. Lynch, grey coat-and-skirted, was
slim as a girl with the pale, narrow face of a
blonde bird. She carried an attaché case and
bowed slightly with closed eyes at every
affirmative.

"Can you make soufflés, puff pastry, crème
brûlée, can you roast well?"

Her mouth closed tight over the secret of
her replies. She breathed affirmatively and
bowed.

"Can you manage your staff?" (Foolish,
hopeless question.)

Mrs. Lynch leant slightly forward.

"Do you get on well with the staff
generally?"

A whiff of air passed her lips.

"You have had your training in the kitchen
always?"

Mrs. Lynch replied defensively that she had
been a temporary for many years. Looking

very intelligent and very treacherous she now raised her eyes. By that the squire knew it was time to make her decision, or this thin and secret bird would be flown and only the branch left waving behind her. She sighed.

"Could you cook the lunch to-day and fetch your suitcase in the afternoon? Can I telephone for your references?"

Mrs. Lynch replied that the "office" held the references. She had an apron in her attaché case; the deal was done; the "temporary," like a wedge-headed serpent, crept into the roots of the house.

Ruby, the kitchenmaid, looked at her as she went upstairs to her room.

"Smart, isn't she?" she said to Queenie.

"Nice costume," said Queenie. "Fits her. Got a figure."

"Gotta sort of poor face," said Ruby, "in front."

"Better'n wearing it on her back hair," said Queenie tartly.

Ruby looked at her, cross and tired from her dance.

75

Mrs. Lynch, installed in the kitchen in a white overall, her fair hair nicely waved, drawn like a madonna's from a central parting round her lean young head, looked out on this new world and drew her knitting from her case. She was knitting a jumper.

"Nice stitch," said Ruby, without admiration.

"Yes," said Mrs. Lynch. "What's a place like?"

"Like everywhere else," said Ruby, "except there's going to be a baby."

"So I saw," said Mrs. Lynch. "I've no objection."

"The last one had. Gave her the shivers. She was queer!"

"Doesn't give me the shivers. S'long as it doesn't happen to me."

"Go on!" said Ruby, and laughed. But she coughed a little to draw her laugh into a neutral region. ("She's got a face like a cracker," thought Ruby. "Not that I care.")

"What's ordered?" said Mrs. Lynch.

76

"It's in the book," said Ruby, sauntering to the table by the window.

"Cutlets," she read. "Open lemon-curd tart."

"Is the stuff here?" said Mrs. Lynch, her needles flying.

Ruby picked up a piece of folded grease-paper and shook the cutlets on to a plate.

"Better get on and trim 'em," said Mrs. Lynch, glancing at the clock.

Ruby looked at her with her underlip out for twenty seconds.

"Are the vegetables on?" said the knitter.

Ruby, fuddled as to her line of action, took the lid off a dark green mass in a sea of water.

"Spinach," she said disdainfully.

"I'm going out after lunch," said Mrs. Lynch. "Mr. Lynch's fetching me suitcase and meeting me on the beach. You better come too, at three. I'm going to put my ankles in the salt water. You'll like Mr. Lynch; he'll take us into the café till tea. Is there cakes made?"

"The drawing-room don't always have

cakes. She don't like 'em much. There's a bit of sponge if anyone comes. The nursery's got theirs. Made yesterday." Ruby pulled a trimming knife from the table drawer.

"The *Nurse* is coming to-morrow," volunteered Ruby.

The jumper leapt round for a new row of stitches in the able hands.

"That's why Mrs. Pascoe left," went on Ruby. "She 'created'. Last night after dinner."

The leaning face watched the knitting as it quivered. "'Created', did she?" murmured the thin lips. "That would be her change, would it?"

Ruby stared, enlightened. "She's about at that," she assented. "I never thought of that."

"Most cooks are at their change," said the lips. "Seems curious. I believe in a bit of sex myself. Keeps you steady."

"What a lot you must get to see, going around," said Ruby admiringly.

"Yes," said the lips, and the knitting sank and lay. Ruby, looking up, was surprised to

see a pair of eyes like knives where the large
pale lids had been.

The squire, for whom this simple meal was
being prepared, was growing hungry.

CHAPTER FIVE

ALONE AND IN THE LIBRARY AFTER LUNCH the squire bent down and lit the paper in the grate beneath the sawn tips from the new chestnut fence. Pratt put the coffee tray on a little stool.

Henry came in quietly and threw things on the new fire while his mother drank her coffee. He had brought a pinch of salt with him and it burnt blue in the flame. He took sugar from the coffee tray and threw that too. Then he fetched bay leaves from the bottom branches of the tree below the terrace. Old bay leaves go off like squibs in a fire.

"Where's Boniface?" said the squire.

"He's in the dining-room. I saw him when I fetched the salt."

At that, the door opened and in came Boniface.

"Come along in, darling," said the squire.

"I have," said Boniface.

Henry was like Lucy. He turned suddenly and said, "How long have you got before you die?"

The squire would have no nonsense with this little child. "I promise you," she said firmly, "another forty years of my life."

"Forty YEARS!" said Boniface with horror. "You'll be an OLD THING."

"I'll be eighty-four," said the squire blenching. "What's the matter with eighty-four?"

Jay came, and rolled billiard balls on the floor under a tunnel of opened books. Over the billiard table lay the great cloth last brought from India, with beetles' green wings embroidered into the pattern with gold threads. This they were forbidden to take off.

Under a glass dome on a side-table stood a model in brass and iron of an old smooth-bore field-gun and limber, sixteen inches long. It had been hand-made by a native Head Armourer of the Arungabad Division of the Nizam's Army of 1838.

"When can I have the field-gun to play with on the floor?" asked Henry for the hundredth time.

"Not till Daddy comes home," said the squire mechanically.

"Why not, why not, why not . . ." said Henry, not questioning but protesting.

Lucy came and read in a deep chair.

"May I make a fire on the terrace? In a flower-pot?" asked Henry.

"You're too young!" said Boniface, startling Henry, who frowned.

"I must pin your front hair back," said the squire. "And strike the matches away from you."

"TOO YOUNG!" said Boniface again in a voice like thunder.

"Lucy!" called the squire, "help him with his fire."

"Can't he do his own fire?" said Lucy, reading.

"I'll do it!" said Jay (from desire), and scrambled over the corner of the billiard table.

Jay got a flower-pot that stood on the

terrace and took Henry to the woodshed to look for chips of wood.

"If I could sit here for ever," thought the squire, "watching the children play!" She had slipped herself down from the sofa and now sat on the floor propped on cushions in the sunny doorway to the terrace, sick with sleep. There was a curious warmth in the air. Boniface, behind her, fiddled with the gramophone. "Change the needle," she said drowsily, leaning, half-panting, against the wall. The flowers bloomed around her in their watery vases, stalks coated with bubbles. Up went the tune into the air. Boniface knelt over the box and stared into it: the tune moaned and wept: the squire, back in Paris, shed her great body. Paris air was thin and fine and a blue dawn broke over the markets, an old man played the tune once again on a worn fiddle. Boniface hung over the whirling disc; he with no background but the nursery and the womb looked unmoved into the abyss of the tune. "How in love I was then!" thought the squire and shifted her weight against the wall. The food settling in her on this warm afternoon, a heavy sleep like a soft death overtook her and her head sank upon her breast.

Crash! went the lid of the gramophone. "Couldn't help it," said Boniface, and crawled towards her on all fours, mumbling as he crawled.

"What's that? What's that you're saying?"

"In Irak once——" he said vaguely.

"Where?"

"The patrols for the Frontier. Let me sit by you?"

Dazed, the squire looked at him.

"They have the base at Irak," he said. "They bomb the native villages. It's in my magazine. I'll show it to you."

"Where is it?"

"In my bedroom. Can someone get it? Can Lucy get it?"

"Why me?" said Lucy.

"I'll show you the printing. What it says."

"Well I will," said Lucy, "because I've got to go up anyway and get my stuff.'

"What stuff?"

"What I have to have. Where is it?"

"In my room I said."

Jay brought a newspaper with a bundle of chips, Henry clattering round him.

"Show him which is windward," said the squire. "Keep him windward when it lights."

Lucy came back. "It's *not* in your room."

"It *is*."

"It isn't."

"S'under my bed," said Boniface.

"Why didn't you say so," said Lucy and sat down again.

Boniface wandered out towards the fire-pot.

"Go away!" said Henry sharply, lifting his face.

"Keep away!" said Jay, lifting his. They scowled.

Boniface went off round the limit of the terrace, renouncing the intentions that his brothers had divined.

The squire nodded and dozed. When she woke she saw through the doorway in the sky a look of thunder. Jay had got the hose and stuck it through the garden seat so that the

water rose at an angle into the green sky. Jay,
Lucy and Henry, their clothes off, were rushing
in and out of the outer spray. The squire, from
sleep, from food, from the tune she had slept
on, from sloth, indolence, happiness, felt her
life fixed and hanging like a shining ball. Love
in the past was nothing as she watched her
children.

The flowers stood stiff in the border, the sky
shone between indigo clouds. The tulips
dripped from the hose, the paths swam in wet
mud, and Jay with a scream rushed into the
force of the water, wearing a streaming, laughing face and hair like a wet bird.

Nurse came for them.

"You've got someone then?" said Nurse.

"I got a temporary," said the squire yawning.

"She's off all ready," said Nurse, sniffing.

"How d'you mean 'off all ready'?" said the
poor squire sharply, sitting upright.

"Just gone down to bathe. The very first
afternoon. An' taken the kitchenmaid."

"Oh, never mind, never mind," said the
squire, relapsing.

"If *you* don't mind," said Nurse. "She'll be a bad influence." And she collected the children for the beach.

"I'm not going," said Lucy.

"Why not?"

"I'm too old. I loathe the beach."

"Loathe the beach!" said Nurse, shocked.

"I'm too old. Digging and digging an' the the sea comes in and wipes it out."

Nurse looked at Lucy. "That's not the way to think," she said.

The children went. With difficulty the squire wiped out the stains that Nurse had left on her mind. Why should Mrs. Lynch be bathing already? She changed her position, contemplated a row of apple shrubs that she had put in last autumn at the bottom of the terrace, and slowly filled up again with comfortable thoughts. Things were coming to a head. Her inner life, her restless inner life, was still and lay asleep. She was at liberty now to think of material things; positions of wardrobes and chests-of-drawers; lists of books to be piled by her bed; dressing-jackets; white woolly vests and pants. It was not often she could thus play dolls and dolls-houses without feeling she ought to be doing something else; that life was short; that she was threatened by the melancholy of life itself, whose vapours sometimes reached her with overpowering strength. From her present sea-deep content two things were absent now—the horror of the ultimate departure, and the need to express herself before the end. The baby seemed to swim and strike like a dolphin. "It is a mystery," she said. "Women bearing children, bulbs becoming hyacinths, acorns . . . sheep . . . lambs. Feet that never touched the earth . . . I shall become two people." She stared between the apple trees; hypnotised, drugged by that sea-deep peace; wonder drifting weedily in and out. She was a vase, a container, a split oak for a gnome to live in, a split oak, a hollow elm.

She pulled herself together while the afternoon hung round her, and rising rearranged a few flowers, adding some early roses the gardener had brought in.

"I've come back," said Boniface, reappearing.

"Why aren't you on the beach?"

"I thought I wouldn't go," he said beginning to walk in circles.

"Keep still. Don't go round and round. Did you run away from her?"

"It wasn't under the bed," he said. "It was under the pillow." He held out his crumpled magazine.

"Oh, Boniface, where have you come from!"

"I'll read it to you. Page nine six."

Standing up beside her he read some of the article aloud, stammering a little, his hair falling over his red face, while she finished the roses.

"Wonderful," said the squire absently. "How well you read now." Then, as she put the last rosebud in a small green vase, "Isn't that a lovely one?"

Boniface came alive and looked alertly at the rose.

"I hate flowers," he said with vigour, and disappeared again, through the window.

*　　　*　　　*　　　*

When the squire took Henry into the nearest town to the toyshop Henry wanted the world. He ran from toy to toy like a kitten after dry leaves, pouncing, relinquishing, and pouncing again. He wept with longing, he frowned, grew white, groaned with the injustice of every refusal and whined all the way home. But Boniface, eyes starting out of his head with interest, wanted nothing. He stood fixed and stared, shook his head at what he was offered, moving slowly from one thing to another. But no, he did not want them. No, no, he did not want them. Why?

Occasionally, very rarely, there was something Boniface desired to possess. Then he would signal, with pursed lips, nodding yes he wanted that. And the squire never denied him. It would be a modest want. Wrapped up, Boniface took the parcel and was lost to all else. He had found, after months, what satisfied him. Sometimes, after such a find, he could not even digest the next meal—(that food the fools had given him, knowing no better than to feed Boniface when he was too happy,

too excited, too closed against fish and suet)—
and literally sick from satisfaction he would lie
in his bed, his red face drained of blood, unable
to stir his head, his treasure perched on the
corner of the chest of drawers, waiting with
speechless patience for the dizzy misery to pass.

Every development and conclusion in Boniface was unheralded. He would not speak, he
would not warn. Only now and then, to the
squire, his face would light up and his awkward
magnificent words would totter out, pompous,
glittering, antique and biblical, past his unsmil-
ing lips and beneath his intent, fixed eyes.
Henry gay and crisp, lived beside Boniface as
on the side of a volcano; ready to dodge and
flee when danger rumbled, knowing that under
the calm and greening slopes God and the
devil lived within, shrugging his creamy
shoulders, grinning when he could, but deeply,
profoundly respectful, as we are all respectful,
towards singleness of purpose, silence, and
absence of explanation.

Henry was often tiresome but deeply wanted
to be good. Boniface did not want to be good,

because he did not think of himself. He
appeared to deal, when he spoke, in harsh
facts, outlandish truths, coffee outputs, depth
soundings, the pull of the tide in the Mediter-
ranean, but the squire was not sure that that
was the fathom of his underground life. Such
things erupted, but beneath again was a layer
of something more unified, a study on which
he was engaged, an encyclopædia of facts. He
cared to *know*. But he did not care who knew
he knew. Sometimes, facing his mother, he
would talk firmly and securely, and then it was
that the marching sentence, whose passage
nothing could hinder, seemed to have been
pre-constructed in steel links under his mind.

He did not like to be disturbed. He liked
to lie and think, lie and read, thumb a catalogue, a telephone directory, a dictionary.
When he was disturbed (as he was disturbed
all day long—to walk, clean his teeth, eat,
go to bed), he would scream. Scream, and
continue to read. And the squire, passing a
door and hearing the noise, would speak to
him with slow disfavour, while he suspended

his noise, resentful, ready to continue. But no,
she would not have that. She knew him and
she probed him and undid his defences and
wrappings. Then finding himself on his beam
ends and unable to delay obedience he would
relax and walk off to his destination.

Under his factual life there were winds veer-
ing and blowing, tides pulling, tides ebbing.
His mother watched and guessed.

CHAPTER SIX

THE SQUIRE WALKED ACROSS THE VILLAGE Green and laid her hand on Caroline's gate. She paused a moment wondering if she wanted to go in.

"I see you!" called Caroline, from a top window.

"What are you doing?"

"Looking to see if the sea is rough."

The squire went in and sat on a deck-chair by the square patches of geranium.

"Why do you let him do this?" she said as Caroline came on to the lawn.

"What? The geraniums?"

"You could tell him you hate them. Tell him *I* hate them."

"He puts them in every year before I come down here."

"Make him take them out."

"I'm thinking of going to Paris."

"Oh . . . Caroline!"

"I'm restless, restless. What is here is stale. What is in Paris is new."

"It's all the same," said the squire, grinning like a Buddha.

"Oh . . . look at you! You're out of it! Nobody was more in, once. But look at you! Children inside and children outside, and children in your mind. Where are they?"

"Gone for a walk. I came over to you. Talk to me about love!"

"So that you can say to yourself how much better than I you can do without it!"

"Something like that," assented the squire, and rocked herself round to ease a sudden stitch. Caroline brooded, her face bent towards the geraniums. "In the long run give me women every time!" she said.

"Nonsense," said the squire, suddenly worried with wind. After meals, what with the baby, there was so little room.

"Why should it be nonsense?"

"You're a love-woman," said the squire. "You're made to please. It's your relation with life, to please. You even please the male in me; you charm everyone; that's how you have fun. But more fun with men."

"Men are a different race."

"Yes, a different race. When I was a girl I fought against that. I couldn't understand why it should be. I thought it was a question of a few years of sex. But it's deeper than that. It comes from centuries of domination. You can *never* break it. You see it in stags!"

Caroline pealed with laughter, thinking of the genial and absent Dominator in Bombay. "You haven't had so much domination!"

"Not so much," said the squire, considering. "But I'm getting older and tougher. But there! I'm getting more male, that's all! I'm the stag myself."

"I should die," said Caroline slowly, "if I had to admit to myself that I had finished with love."

There was nothing to say to that.

"You are far, very far from it," said the

squire. "You'll go on looking beautiful for ever."

"And change of life?"

"Oh, that's a joke! Look at the world's old mistresses! History is peppered with saucy old women."

Caroline winced.

"It isn't a question of Age," the squire went on. "It's a passage. Continually a passage. New and disturbing phenomena. Ceasing, ceasing to want things. Ceasing to want things. Put your face into it and glower into it. You *cease to want things*. There is a kind of savage joy," said the squire, "in getting to the end of the pleasures of youth."

"When does your midwife come?" said Caroline.

"M'm . . ." said the squire, absent. "What? To-night."

"To-night? No more evenings together?"

"How often have we had them? She comes to-night."

"You look as though *you* were in love!" said Caroline suddenly.

97

"Have I that look? I feel expectant, excited. It's a closing-in, and the moment is coming nearer and nearer."

"How near?"

"Things are going to happen," said the squire, impatiently. "I'm cramped. I'll have to walk about. Good God, I can hardly stand!"

She got up, pressing her belly with her hands.

"Where are you going?"

"Back to nail up some creepers, and potter. I want to get the room ready, flowers, for the midwife. And look at the cradle and potter." She walked towards the gate. "I'm so stupid, Caroline, I can hardly talk. I'm only a shell. Did I look 'in love'? Perhaps I looked 'entranced'. To-night with the midwife's coming I go into the last period, a purification. Stripped of my children, accompanied by a nun, and all the cares of the household thrust from me! Soon, one morning or one night, I shall turn from all daily companionship to the 'monk' and the 'nun' . . . and do under their direction those medieval acrobatics which are to turn this aged and silent creature inside me into a young and crying child."

"I shan't go to Paris till you've had it," said Caroline suddenly. "*He* shall come across to me!"

"Oh, I shouldn't wait, I shouldn't change anything!"

"Not for your sake. You're all right, so tough and clever! But I want to see the baby the minute it's born. I want to be sure I don't envy you."

"You won't be allowed in, with your charming 'evil-eye'!"

"What do you mean?"

The squire chuckled. "You don't know my midwife. She's psychic. She'll know you're a love-woman. She won't let you bend over her newborn."

"Stop calling me that!" said Caroline. "It's revolting. Aren't you the least afraid?"

"No. Not this time. Sometimes I play with death in my head, but it means nothing. Sometimes I plan the herbaceous border and pretend I think I shall never see it flower. But it means

nothing. I never was so free from fear.
Normally, while I live, while I walk, while I
talk, I can smell death like the scent in a handkerchief held to my nose. Now it's gone.
No . . . no. This is the fifth birth, and I'm
more collected, more ready to watch. I know
every step. I know that from to-night I'm
heading straight, with an impresario beside me.
Like a boxer with his trainer. Nothing left to
chance, nothing haphazard. Then when the
moment comes, we gather together as for a
race. The pace quickens, there is excitement,
I have my central, stoic part to play—the monk
and the nun, my attendants, my leaders, like
a couple of archangels!

"And you see," she went on, hitching one
hip onto the low cobble-wall, "the first time
is all panic. The second half-panic, but at the
third and fourth times something began to
dawn on me. I said, 'Is this really *pain*'?"

"But it's frightful, isn't it?"

" 'Is this really *pain*'," said the squire
impatiently, " 'or is it an extraordinary
sensation'?"

"What's the difference?"

"Pain is but a branch of sensation. Perhaps child-birth turns into pain only when it is fought and resisted? I'm aching, I'm restless, I can't tell you now. But there comes a time, after the first pains have passed, when you swim down a silver river running like a torrent, with the convulsive, corkscrew movements of a great fish, threshing from its neck to its tail. And if you can *marry* the movements, go with them, turn like a screw in the river and swim on, then the pain . . . then I believe the pain . . . becomes a flame which doesn't burn you."

"Awful!" said Caroline, shuddering.

"It's not awful. The thing's progressive. And when you are right *in* the river to marry the pain requires tremendous determination, and will, and self-belief. You have to rush ahead into it, not pull back against it. It's very hard to do."

"Did you manage it last time?"

"No. But I got moments. And they were very clear afterwards. It's clear to me now. I know what I've got to do, if I can only keep my head. It must be the secret of child-bearing in the past, when women had eleven and fifteen children and learnt how to have them. Only most of us don't get enough practice . . . Lucy! Lucy! What are you doing?"

"I've come back to look for Boniface. Nurse sent me."

"He's in the house. He never went with Nurse. Find him."

Lucy went. The front door of the other house banged across the Green.

"I must go and potter, Caroline. Walk across with me."

"What's that!" Caroline stopped short.

Screams poured from the nursery windows opposite. The squire hurried a little. Then Lucy came through the front door, serene, carrying something under her arm. The yells died slowly down into a wailing.

"What's the matter?" asked the squire.

"Boniface has torn all the date-cards off my calendar I made."

"What have you done? Did you hit him?"

"I've taken his atlas away. For a week."

"A whole week, Lucy!" said the squire aghast. (Boniface could not live half a day without his atlas.)

Lucy looked at her. "I *said* a week," she said. "He doesn't know what a week means. I'll give it back to him after tea."

"I'll stick your date-cards in again," said the squire beaming at her. "Good girl. *Good* girl."

"I'm trying to be good," said Lucy. And walked off towards the sea.

"I am frightened of the young," said Caroline, watching her go.

"But the young do not remain young. They too are doomed!" And Caroline turned back and the door of her own house slammed behind the squire.

She met Boniface coming from the nursery stairs, his face swollen, his eyes wet, but his expression calm.

"What have you done?" said the squire.

"Nothing," said Boniface, and trudged along.

"Why have you been crying?"

Boniface turned and looked at her. He seemed to reflect. "I've been yelling," he said briefly, and left her.

The thunderous light of the earlier afternoon still lingered about, and down at the sea it lit the shore. The paddling bodies on the fringe of the incoming tide glittered as they moved. Old women's pallid faces turned green in the strange aquarium sunlight, and the naked children shone like buttery metal.

Mrs. Lynch and Ruby giggled in the water and held up their skirts. Mr. Lynch sat on the beach with his hat cocked over one eye and wound the guinea gramophone. Mr. Lynch was no more Mr. Lynch than Ruby's eye, and Ruby knew as much. So he added a spice to the moment, being anybody's game. The water tickled and tinkled round Ruby's fat, white, veinous legs and she looked enviously at Mrs. Lynch's elegant knees with the skirt bound skittishly above them. Ruby's knees were like hocks, but she had a broad, amorous face and

was pop-eyed and gay. The water glittered
and poured in cascades into fresh pools as the
tide came up. Mr. Lynch screamed shrilly as
the water flowed near him and moved further
up the beach. The silvery stuff followed yet
again as the height of the tide approached, and
Ruby was obliged to hold her skirts higher
still. When the tide was near battering on the
cliffs they left the beach and went up to the
Café.

"What's yours?" said Mr. Lynch gallantly
to Ruby.

"Vanilla-cone," said Ruby.

"Haven't you got shorts?" said Mrs. Lynch.
"I'll bring mine over to-morrow."

"Her ladyship stopped the last nurserymaid
wearing shorts," said Ruby.

"Pooh!" said Mrs. Lynch. "What a nerve!
Did the girl give in her notice?"

"Well, so she did. But she stayed on. She
wants to be there when the baby's born."

"What's that butler like?" said Mrs. Lynch.

"Him? Gloomy. Awful in the mornings."

"Men are like that, aren't they, Johnny?"

Mr. Lynch let one eyelid down and hauled it up again.

Slowly the bathers passed the café, going up after the high tide, long-coated in towelling, the dripping rags they had worn swinging in their hands.

"Soon be tea-time," said Mrs. Lynch.

"Beats me," said Ruby, "how you can walk into a house and ask no questions an' take it all on."

Mrs. Lynch's eyes narrowed. She asked no questions because Ruby, under the flattery of the afternoon with Johnny would take everything on for her. Nothing like a good kitchen-maid if she could only be kept "running on." Ruby "knew the ways," Ruby would run on like a clock. She had to be managed, pushed, flattered, and prodded. Mr. Lynch would give her a friendly slap and a whisper if need be, if she showed signs of flagging. Mrs. Lynch would give her a look, if need be. That very evening Mrs. Lynch intended "slipping back to town" while Ruby roasted the duckling. She would be back by midnight and Ruby would sit up willingly, so long as Johnny came too and they had a secret meal all three before he had to return. With half an eye, on her arrival in the kitchen, Mrs. Lynch could see that fat Ruby was a good one if jollied up and kept going.

"Those are our children!" said Ruby suddenly with pleasure.

Nurse pushed the victoria in which Henry was seated, his bare feet hanging over. Lucy and Jay went past. Ruby was fond of them and saved them scraps and bones for their dogs.

"That nurse'll have her work cut out," remarked Mrs. Lynch.

Ruby looked at her in surprise. "She's potty about the new one. She can't hardly wait. Every day when she comes in from her walk she asks as she goes through the back door if anything's begun."

"Strange way of talking. Indecent I call it," said Mrs. Lynch.

"Well, when you live with it . . ." said Ruby, defending herself and Nurse.

"Have another cone?" said Johnny, lifting

his feet up on to a chair and shutting one eye
after the other like a lean owl.

"Lay off!" said Ruby, and laughed her jolly
laugh. "Them cones is terrible," and she took
a bunch of fat on her hip with her hand and
shook it at them. She wobbled all over
through her thin muslin dress. ("They're a
pair of queers" she said to herself. "I don't
know as I'm so set on them.")

("Common," thought Mrs. Lynch. "Knowing life's one thing, but common's another."
And her mysterious face, half adder, half
madonna, gazed out to sea through the café
window panes.)

"I'll have to punish Boniface," thought
Nurse, as she jolted the pram over the step
into the side yard.

"What are you going to do to Boniface?"
asked Lucy who had fits of thought-reading.

"That's my business," said Nurse.

"I should think," said Lucy, "if you kept
him out of the sandpit for a day it would be
a good punishment."

"*I* need him in the sandpit," said Jay

instantly. "He's fetching cans of water for me to pour down the tunnel."

"Kitchen's stone empty," said Nurse, as they passed the open kitchen door. "I *thought* I saw them both in the café. Who's to do the eggs for tea?"

"Make him have *two* boiled eggs," said Jay, pursuing the punishment. "Underdone."

"Make him eat all our egg-whites," said Lucy with a shudder.

"That's enough," said Nurse. "And you, Jay, not another word. I have quite enough trouble over eggs. First who's to cook 'em, and when they're cooked who's to eat 'em?"

"Then why try?" said Jay.

The squire had seen them from a window. Her pulse beat quicker at the sight. Suddenly, as they walked with their buckets, it was not the child in each face that she sought, but the Wonder that had raised itself on to its two feet, that had learnt to walk, to run, that had spoken, that had got in touch with life under her hand. She burned with pride, inwardly shaken with wonder. That the Newborn in each child had come up the dangerous path from birth to this! Those embryos, those hanging sea-urchins, see how magnificently now they walked up the street, buckets in hand!

"Lucy, Lucy, Jay, Jay, Henry!" she called.

"There's your mother calling," said Nurse crossly. It was trying, the way the squire would call and scatter them when she had just got them headed up the staircase to be washed for tea.

CHAPTER SEVEN

THE GOOD SQUIRE, THE GREEDY OLD BIRD, had a sense of last-minute freedom. The midwife would be here in half an hour and the laws of the last stages would be laid upon her. It was outrageous to drink a glass of port at tea-time, but she made off to the dining-room sideboard to soak her sponge-cake in port for tea.

"Fancies," she said to herself. "I must have my fancies!"

Now having eaten her soaked sponge-cake, and having put flowers most joyfully in the midwife's bedroom, she went off down the village street to meet her, walking lightly for all her enormous bulk.

The midwife was still sitting in the bus, rocking between the sea and the dunes, propped up upon the high road with the blue vegetation bursting through the sand below. She had left her luggage for the carrier at the station. Now she laid her fine hands one over the other on her leather bag and looked out to sea, thinking of her errand, thinking of possibilities, methods, difficulties. A journey for this purpose she had made so many, many times before, but never without this inner trembling of ecstasy. Her light blue eyes took on the colour of the sea.

They were old hands, she and the squire. This was the fifth time they had worked together. She knew the squire had laid her ground well and was in fine condition, brown as a light loaf from head to foot, and strong. The midwife's face, as she looked at the sea, was beautiful as a window; the spirits sat in it but she had learnt how to hold them steady. She had no need in this case for her resolutions and her armour. The squire could be disciplined and good. She expected a gallant and peaceable baby, yet something rigid, fierce and bright lay ready in her crouching armed against disturbance, ready to crush what tampered with the harness of her routine. Upright, she was out of the ordinary tall, her hair was red and curled up from her forehead. She had that Scotch expression, sweet and harsh, bony and feminine, high-coloured and high cheek-boned, pale eyes concentrated and infinitely observant. Her skin flushed easily, and when her eyes flashed it was as though she had taken up a sword.

The midwife was a Religious and a crusader. If the future was threatened the fur flew. And this was what the squire liked. From now on she left her body and her baby in these unquestioned hands. The squire in her good-humoured greed and comfortable wisdom was gay in company with this eagle, chuckled to see intruders driven off her, to see herself keyed up, rolled like a tumbrel of good wine upon a narrow plank of virtue.

She was late, the bus at the end of the street had rocked to a standstill and the midwife had got out. The squire came sailing like a ship in the distance, and waved. They hurried to meet each other, the squire in excitement and love, out of breath, pressed on to meet her.

"Safe!" thought the squire. "Now it can start when it likes!" She felt rolled up on an ocean shore by a last gigantic lop of sea. "Poof! . . . Safe! Heigho . . ." She ambled back beside her friend, shining with pleasure and relief.

"Where have you come from?"

"I handed over a baby yesterday evening."

"A nice baby?"

"Yes," said the midwife with a sigh.

They reached the house and Pratt stood in the doorway with a look of rueful and unwilling pleasure on his face. The midwife met his eyes, straight, and he smiled. Grumble he did but he could not resist this woman. Time and again she had been here. This made the fifth. Each time he had maligned her before her arrival, and the first time he had carried on a low warfare over some trifle but in the very first breath he was beaten. She knew her job, she knew his job, a good woman (he admitted) and a lady. Strict. Never let

114

anything pass. He had felt cross all day about her arrival, but now she was here a sober welcome came up from his curious heart, and he smiled, a dark man's smile, with a faint purpling blush on his blue cheek.

"And wasn't it a nice baby?" said the squire over her second tea, "or was it the nurse that was wrong."

"The household was wrong," said the midwife sadly. "Or perhaps it was the mother, poor thing. Last night I prayed to the saints for the baby." Alone in her hired room she had prayed to the saints for the baby. Not to God; she never prayed to God; she had this strange feeling about the saints.

"What sort of a mother?" asked the squire.

"I try to be fair," said the midwife, leaning back. "As I am not married there must be difficulties into which I can't enter."

"You mean the husband kept saying, 'Don't feed the brat! You'll spoil your lovely figure. You'll make your breasts droop! Remember, you're *mine!*'"

There was a short silence.

"How is it possible for *me* to enter into *that?*" asked the midwife of herself. "As I grow older I come to consider men . . . husbands of women, husbands of mothers . . . as hindrances to my work."

"You wouldn't get your work without them."

"No. But more and more I feel they should be absent, kept back from the moment of birth."

"Ah, no," said the squire remembering. "It's sweet to wake up from it all and be applauded by a husband. The little dinners in the bedroom, the fading light, the baby brought in at ten. . . ."

"You see how limited I am!" smiled the midwife moving long fingers in a gesture of her own. "Because I am not married I am specialised, and I find it difficult to brook (even beautiful) hindrances that come in the way of my babies. But in the case of the baby I have left there was nothing very beautiful. The man was selfish, the woman lazy, they were rich, spoilt in health and temper, and now about to spoil another human being."

"Did you tell them so?"

A slow blush rose in the midwife's sensitive skin. "It was not my work to tell them so, but to do what I could for the baby in the life it is to have."

"But you *did* tell them so?"

"I did."

As she said this her eyes blazed. She felt the sword in her hand, she was all for achievement and none for compromise.

"Tell me from the beginning," said the squire, putting up her feet. "Tell me more."

"From the very beginning it went wrong," said the midwife.

She had been at her case at three o'clock, flushing as she touched the doorbell, flushing as the footman opened the door, and saying to him, "I am the trained nurse." Trouble was immediately upon her on the threshold. Disruption, disunity, disharmony showed in the manner of the footman as he dumped her bag in the hall. Once in her room, barely distenanted from its last owner, smudged with faint leavings, she said to herself "Does the spirit of the household reach from the front door to the nursery?" A curling-tongs stood on the window-sill, a dressing-gown hung on the door, and the bed linen and the pillow-case were clean, but not the bolster.

Trembling at the insult to her profession she walked to the window where she could see across the roofs a group busy at a late meal in a chauffeur's room above a mews, a father in his shirt-sleeves, a mother with a dish, and three young children sitting at a table.

Watching them, transported, her hand on the sill, she drew from her jacket pocket a little book and held it in her hands. The words in it were known to her. She did not pray or read. Unsure of the existence of God she thought instead of St. Francis of Assisi, and that he stood behind her and touched her hair. The humble family across the roofs had broken her ferocity. "Sacrifice," she murmured. "Humility."

Others might have endured the dirt in the

room with humour, with philosophy, or from habit. To her it was a dishonour, and as such brought out her sainthood. She, called to the newborn, should have been housed in cleanliness and in reverence. Her job was delicate, dangerous, holy. She should have slept on an altar to perform it. If this room was dirty in her dishonour then the servants would be insolent, the service difficult, the arrival of the baby tarnished. These people did not understand. "Help me," she whispered to St. Francis, "to blow into this house the wind of expectation. Help me, to discipline them." Going from case to case she expected the perpetual arrival of Christ.

Changing into her uniform, coifing her head, she went down to the mother.

"And then?" said the squire, "and the mother?"

"I have been in houses," said the midwife sternly, sitting upright, "where the mother drank or was a kept woman, but never where there was no maternity, never where the woman, whatever her habits, was not moved by this event. This woman put her sex before her maternity. Her husband backed her up. They two were agreed, and before me, that the pleasure she could give a man came before the baby that was to be born to her."

"But why did she have the babies?"

"Let us not speak of it," said the midwife. And the squire knew that the midwife had spent the weeks behind her alternately in battle and on her knees, kneeling in self-battle, rising temporarily victorious, returning to her humiliation and her work.

"Some day," said the squire, "you will be helped to your dream. A convent-clinic, where nuns abet the mothers. And birth is worshipped. What a mother-superior you would make!"

"A convent-clinic!" said the midwife. "Why even a cat is left undisturbed in the stable after birth."

"Because she might eat her young! We aren't as dramatic as that!"

"The world eats the chances of the young," replied the midwife. "How seldom I can care for a mother and her baby in the peace I want for my work, away from the household and its surroundings! My clinic would be a palisaded place, far in the country. There the mother should travel beforehand, passing through the isolation of a journey, leaving husband and family with their pre-occupations in the world. There, in a camp, like an athlete in training she should do her work for the newborn out of sight of life. No legends, no nonsense. The highest medical efficiency. Pre-natal observations carried out . . ." she raised her eyes with a jerk from the wink of the silver tea-tray. "Even a cat," she repeated, "is left undisturbed!"

"Perhaps so," said the squire ruminating. "I know I feel like Gulliver sometimes, weighed down by little men. There are so many people in this house, I'm a queen bee, with every muscle dragging. I'm the heart of a cluster, black, dripping, sucking, hanging. They say they can't do without me. But if I died to-morrow they'd cling to something else." There was silence. "The desperation of age!" said the squire suddenly.

"I never feel it," said the midwife, looking straight in front of her.

"You never feel it," said the squire, "because you are a votive creature, all your eyes on your work. I am at middle age, but that's not why I've got my eyes cocked onwards into the future. Lucy is the same. 'I'm ten,' she said this morning. 'I've done a seventh part of my life.' She's like me. She feels time passing like a cord moving in her bowels. She's moved by time, she's shifting. She knows it. Look at me, too. The children rising like expanding columns beside me. Soon they'll be past me and I shall be walking in undergrowth, walking in a wood, sitting in a wood, sinking in a wood, buried in a wood, *gone*. And the trees will fall too, one by one, and . . . *Henry!* . . ."

"Why Henry?"

"Is it possible to bear death, looking at that silver bulb, that baby! Only," said the squire, lightly hitting her belly with her fingers, "only for the embryo have I *no* pity! It needs no pity yet. It isn't born. Isn't it enough to have four creatures in my heart? The one in the womb hasn't cried, hasn't spoken, hasn't looked out at me with its human eye!"

"I've come," said the midwife, looking at the squire with milder eyes, "to deliver it to your pity."

But the squire sat and sat, thinking. The children, seeds on the face of the earth, grew with an electric life. They burst under her eyes, the shoots came out, came up like lances, with a buzz of growing. One in her womb, one in the womb of his babyhood, Boniface in the womb and tangle of his own mind, Jay and Lucy out and away, Jay and Lucy running, bright and clear. Jay with his sweet face, light hair turning brown, his arrogance, flushing tempers, pride and reasonableness, Lucy with deep struck roots like Boniface and like her mother, one eye cocked on the passage of time, hanging fire, watching, paling. "I'm ten. I've done a seventh part of my life."

The midwife knew that the squire's mind was sogged in dream. She let her be and lay back in the corner of the sofa. With her mysteriously-developed instinct, so sharpened by her work, she felt that the baby was gathering itself together for its exit. "It'll be to-night," she felt, though no doctor could positively have said so. She saw the squire's lids close as she sank into a second's sleep, and folding her own long hands she sat back beside her patient. The lamp under the tea-urn was alight but frail in the sunlight. There was a warm peace about the bright and derelict tea-tray, its crumbs, its silence, its air of human use, presided over by the mothy flame. As the squire slipped between sleep and sleepy thought the midwife, sharpened by her premonition, counted her resources. She knew the lie of the house well. Presently she rose like a tall shadow and slipping quietly out of the room she went to the telephone.

*   *   *   *

"Nurse!" she said, looking into the nursery.

Nurse jumping up pushed a cushion into the corner of the sofa.

"I won't sit down, but have you everything

ready? I really think that baby may come to-night."

Nurse, her face transfigured, took the well-worn list from her apron pocket.

"No sleep for me!" said Nurse, announcing a treat.

"No, no. You must go to bed in the ordinary way. Only it seems to me very near."

"Each day I've been saying to myself 'Is it to-day?' When I come in from my walk I expect everything to be at sixes and sevens. Water boiling, the telephone ringing, the maids on the look-out for me. But it's always as usual. I'm so glad to see you!"

"Can I see everything?"

"It's all ready in the nursery, under a dust-sheet. Will you come now?"

Nurse's happy excitement was flying in her face. All her dreams as a young girl of sixteen, all the scrubbing and washing and running to orders that she had done as a nurserymaid, all the years spent in picking up scraps of know-ledge, of working first here and then there, minding the older children, and later on the younger, all had been directed on such a crisis as this. Birth, and the newborn, and her own "sole charge." The elder children stood back a pace, pale hedges in a garden, while she dived like a gardener into the mould to tend the new plant.

Now, showing to the midwife the tools she had sharpened. . . .

CHAPTER EIGHT

DOWNSTAIRS CAROLINE HAD STROLLED IN. The squire, having listened to a new story, was rubbing her hands and walking about.

"The secrets told in love, Caroline! How safe they seem! Why do you *tell* him such things! It's a mania you have. It's your form of being in love. How safe, how safe the secrets seem, told when in love. And the Enchanted, the Immortal, becomes an enemy. Becomes a young man in a blue suit who knows too much about you!"

"Not *this* time!"

"Not *this* time!" said the squire in mockery. "Let's walk in the garden, there's a full moon."

A yellow moon looked over a hedge of yew.

"The grass is wet," said Caroline, but the squire strode on. They sat on a dry seat sheltered from the dew, staring at the low hanging moon, the one lit with a delicate unrest, the other frowning and smiling into the future.

"You oughtn't to be here with me," said the squire. "Where is this young man to-night?" As she said it she put her hands behind her and rested the strained arch in the hollow of her spine. Caroline was silent. The squire's thoughts streamed on. ("Who is this young man? What is love? A glory pouring through a texture. Who is this young man? A mortal who was a baby, who will grow old, who has a business, who buys his pyjamas, who tramples through his days towards no end, a creature beautiful and inspiring for a moment, but mortal like myself! Do I miss it? I cannot remember it. This is age. There were human beings whom I used to hold sacred, who lit me like one who runs into a cavern with a torch. "Madam, I am a magician!" So they are, so they are magicians. There's one been at Caroline . . . like a mouse at the cheese!") The squire chuckled aloud.

"What's that?"

"Gauzy magic. I've eaten too much fruit to-day."

"Aren't you well?"

"A touch of stomach-ache."

"Are you cold out here?"

"No, no, it's gone! Do you know what I'm thinking of? That we two are so different sitting here on one bench! You full of love, but I'm taking a header. Such a header! I've got to split!"

"Don't!" said Caroline, shuddering.

"Well, there it is! That's what I've come to! And I used to be like you, you know."

"Never quite."

"Never as beautiful, never as made for love, never such a victim."

"That's what I meant. Never such a victim. I have seen you discard a man. I have never discarded a man."

"The first time I did that I grew up. I stopped a love affair in full flight and went away, because I wanted myself for myself. I never was the same afterwards. It developed the male in me, the *choosing* streak in me. There is love with tenderness and there is love without tenderness. When you learn that another creature is pitiful, is doomed, that he is one for whom you feel wrung in those empty, sorrowing night hours, then you enter with him a ring fence from which you never can come out. Marriage is like that. Because of pity it becomes so indescribably important. From battles and intimacy and love, through the passage of time and the carrying on of a common life, there springs up a fellow-pity, from the very base of the heart, from our roots striking mystically downwards. I watch my husband and my children," said the squire very low, "and in their situation I see my own.

". . . I see my own" . . . said the squire speaking now to herself. . . . "Aware of the horror and beauty of *my* mortality while I shiver at *theirs*. Heavy, distant rumble of thunder when I watch my husband and my children! Pity, which can be such a weakening, disabling emotion, which can take such a grand shape, which has such weapons, which is almost divine. That deep, terrible feeling only

my mother and my husband and my children
have drawn from me. Could any young man
of Caroline's steal in as deep as this? Because
of my *family* (which is more to me than the
outside world), because of them, because of
myself . . . for I have for myself the same
deep, loving emotion, the same aching pity
. . . I have looked so interminably on death.
Like a boy at the end of the holidays, saying
half-consciously, as he wakes and turns in
sleep. 'Only three more days . . . only
two. . . .'

"I glance at the final parting again and again.
I try to accustom myself. I look at those other
creatures, my own, so deeply-known, such
loving hearts; their short lives, their high
quality, their baffled condition, their courage.
Their final doom is there before me: I look at
it, I sort it over, I shiver and I *love*. No young
man ever came near that. No young man
bearing the cup from which Caroline drinks.
My lips used to tremble at its touch, I grew
luminous, I walked about like a torch. But the
light went down. Caroline, beside me, looking

at the moon, thrilling, brooding, impatient, transported, full of secret smiles, full of sentences that already play round the beloved name, full of tranced reflections that grow warm, *I know it all*, but I have lost it, and since I am *another being* I don't miss my loss!"

The moon went higher over the black hedge, losing her yellow light. "Trouble and pain" (said the squire again to herself), "of modern hearts! Mine, soon to be an ancestress! The toil of growth, the pride of middle age, when the sense of beauty dims and the heart is blown about by giant troubles, bigger than beauty."

"*De profundis!* Out of the depths, but of what? Everything is out of the depths. The 'depths' lie round like a Sahara, behind, beyond, before the womb. Reasons are 'out of the depths,' birth, this baby, 'out of the depths.'"

So they sat on and presently Caroline said, "He's crossing the day after to-morrow." And when she said it she thought she had said all poetry. She thought she had described the expectation, the waking in the morning, his nearing excitement over the waves of the Channel, the music of the hour while she dressed for him, the summer shine of the moment when, the car coming to the door, she started to meet him. She thought all this was hanging in the night, twin vision to the moon. But the squire pressed slightly back into the seat and felt again the touch of pain, a finger tweaking her bowels for a second, like the thick cords of a harp thrumming in a wind. It had come and gone. She rose to her feet with a severe look and stood thoughtfully, and Caroline bemused and thinking of her own beauty said she must go to bed. They walked down the lawns and steps together, off the high ground, and again the squire paused as though listening.

"Did you hear a child crying?" said Caroline.

"No," said the squire.

When Caroline had gone the squire went round the house as usual, glad to be rid of the beautiful woman. She was trembling with excitement, and her head swam. She tapped at the door of her heart and looked inside. "Fear in there?" she asked. But the room was empty. No fear anywhere. Was this the moment? Had they arrived together, she and the child, at the parting? She was uncertain and would not call the midwife. Instead, she went to her born children, opening and shutting their doors one by one, moving on heavy gentle feet. A light shone under the midwife's door, and voices were talking, Nurse was in there still.

Downstairs she saw to her papers and bills and glanced at the weekly books for payment, standing up with one light burning over her desk in the long empty room, tapping the papers into place, signing her name, passing a bill. Every now and then she looked through the black glass into the night where she had drawn back the curtains, seeming to listen for the pain, staring straight ahead of her, but its touch was so tender she could not pin it down. A thrum of the harp cords came as she moved, and was gone when she stood still.

"What an extraordinary adventure!" she

said aloud suddenly. She did not think of death for a moment, never so absent from the thought of death. The room seemed filled with her excitement, while she listened. So a horse in a loose box hears the hounds on the wind.

*   *   *   *

Two hours later she lay on the sofa with the midwife on her knees beside her, her long, thin hands spread over the naked belly of her patient. The midwife's eyes were shut. She was listening and divining with her hands; then she glanced up at the clock. The night was still; the fire died down. Now and then the midwife spoke, and the squire lay looking at the ceiling and smiling.

"It's very indefinite," said the midwife at last. "I shan't call yet."

"What's your rule of thumb?" said the squire.

"It's hard to say," said the midwife absently, and laid her hands on the mounded belly again.

"Surely this one's definite?" said the squire

presently, her eyes on a fly walking over its shadow on the ceiling.

"Better," said the midwife, and she looked again at the clock.

"Well then?"

"One mustn't call too soon, one mustn't call too late."

"I should think not!"

There were long silences and the curious mediæval picture remained posed. The woman about to go into labour lay, clothed, but her belly exposed, thrilled, and silent, holding in her silence the very centre of a lively stage. The other actor, with her centuries of tradition, on her knees, listening with her slender hands for the creak of the gates that would open to let out her charge. If the shade of the window-cleaner had returned to his black window in the dead of night he would have seen a group, indecent, venerable, moving, blessed by antiquity.

At last the midwife rose and looked down in thought. "I shall call him," she said. "Warn him. It will be hours yet."

"Oh!" said the squire. "We'll get this baby out before dawn breaks! Let's look at the sky." She rose and crossed to the french windows and stooped to pull up the bolts. A smell of cigarette came in from the street beyond the terrace with the smell of flowers and the cold smell of earth.

"Shall I wake Pratt?" she asked. "To make sure the boiler is going?"

"If you like," said the midwife, giving her something to do.

So the squire toiled up the stairs, pausing outside the open day-nursery door to let a touch of pain go by and leave her. She climbed yet another flight and tapped at a door. There was no sound and she tapped again, then heard the click of the electric light and opened the door. Within lay Pratt, on his back, his eyes open, and at sight of her his instinct was to draw the sheet modestly to his neck.

"Are you awake, Pratt? I have started the baby," said the squire simply. "I thought you'd like to be called. There will be things to do, the telephone, and to see the boiler is going."

He assented willingly, from over the top
of the drawn-up sheet. He would not move
till she had gone.

"May I wish your ladyship well?" he said as
she reached the door. The victim of the coming
storm smiled back at him. How clever, how
correct, how almost sweet he was, on such
rare moments!

"And now?" said the squire, reaching her
bedroom, where she heard the midwife moving.

"Now I should go to bed. Undress and go
to bed."

"To bed?" said the squire disgustedly,
sniffing at the night air through the open
window.

"I should go. You may doze. You may
sleep it quiet again and then it will be daylight
and no need to wake the household."

"This is a Birth!" said the squire. "Let the
household wake! But I'll lie down for a little.
I shan't sleep."

She lay down waiting on the vague pains,
and presently slept.

When she woke the doctor was opening

her door. The midwife was behind him.

"The monk and the nun!" thought the squire and twisting, caught her breath. "Bad one coming!" she gasped, and pain surged up her back.

"You're to get up as soon as you've been looked at. Get up and dress and have your breakfast," said the midwife.

The squire snuggled down defiantly in bed. "I'm staying here till I have it. The pains will be bad soon. I'm not getting up."

"I've ordered breakfast for three, downstairs in half an hour's time. Mrs. Lynch said she had sausages. Will that be all right?"

Mrs. Lynch! How far, far below was Mrs. Lynch, on the lowest slopes of the mountain of birth!

". . . that caps it," she murmured vaguely as another pain began.

"What?"

"Pleasure . . ." grunted the squire, and shut her eyes. "My pleasure . . . to be here. . . ."

When the doctor had left her the squire got

up and dressed, grumbling, and came downstairs. Queenie, who was in the hall, looked at
her with curiosity and stole away. No one
could address the squire to-day, ask to go to a
dance, or for an evening off, or give her
notice. She was out of it; moving like a ghost
in her own house, her eyes veiled with concentration, coming alive during the respites,
and standing steady and quiet during the pains.
Pratt brought in the coffee and set it down.

"Sausages?" said the doctor drawing in his
chair to the table.

"Where are the children?" said the squire.

"Out till lunch-time," said the midwife.
"Nurse has taken them off."

"Did you tell Lucy and Jay?"

"Lucy knew. She'd guessed."

Where were they now? Walking above the
sea, hitting the blue thistles with a switch,
dragging behind. Walks of children, endless
walks of children, sucking grass to make the
time pass. Nurse ploughing ahead with a
look of secret triumph she could not suppress,
Jay shouting and running, and Lucy quiet. She

saw the four children with a brilliant clarity over the edge of a pain.

The doctor was drinking his coffee with gusto. The squire came back to life, sweating. "It must be near now!"

"Nonsense!" he said. "You women never learn. Got to walk miles before it's nearer."

He began a conversation with the midwife; the squire joined in when she could. She held the edges of the chair-seat with her hands and sweated, then back came life and comfort, and she ate her crisp sausage and nodded to them both. She looked at her doctor and was so filled with trust it was like love.

"Out on to the lawn!" he said, when they had finished their odd meal, "and find me *The Times!*"

"You are staying with me! You're not leaving me!"

"Get me *The Times*, and I'll have a morning off in a deck-chair."

So he lay in a deck-chair, his hat cocked over his nose and turned the big sheets of paper; and now and then he would look round at her and say "Get on! Get on!" The midwife disappeared upstairs on her own errands.

The quiet morning wore on; the maids peeped at her now and then from the windows; the little wood beyond the pond shimmered, the frogs clung to their scraps of buoys winking their copper eyes. The squire walked. She trod slowly, thinking of nothing, swept alternately by beauty and by pain. When the beauty came it was unearthly, because threatened. Her eyes took in the distances beyond the trees, the quantity of light allowed to fill the spaces. She was filled with sight. Then once more came the pain. She paused, leaning against a tree-trunk, while the pain shoved and pressed her from within, swelling and kneading her. *The Times* at the end of the garden never stirred now nor fluttered, as its reader read and read, but counted, too. He knew where she was and what she could stand. "Get on, get on . . ." he murmured. Then the pain ebbed in a slow release and back came the world, lit and cubic, one thing behind another, and light between. Squares and oblongs of solid light. What had gone *right* with her eyes? Was it pain, pressure, a swelling of the blood, that they saw so strangely and so newly-well? She wandered on, till—steady— steady—lean against the tree—for here it comes again! At eleven she made a run for the stairs, the doctor instantly at her side as she sank on the bottom step. "Can't you do another round?"

"No, I can't! I won't. I must get on to my bed."

"Very well."

She went up and once in her room there and the bed near she could afford to walk again. She walked a little longer, anxious to please her doctor. Then, as she lay again on the pillow her face to one side, her hands holding the wooden bed-head she saw the midwife pass the open door of her room to the outer balcony where the cot was standing. Over her arms were blankets for the cot, and under one clenched elbow a hot water-bottle pressed against her waist. Rest and glory filled the squire between the pains. She watched the

preparations for the unborn; watched the
things laid out with which to wash what WAS
NOT THERE, to warm the feet of what
DID NOT BREATHE, the settling of the
pillows and the blankets for what COULD
NOT BE TOUCHED. There she lay, beached
for a moment, panting, quivering, aware.
And now she spoke no more, only savouring
her moments of release; waiting for the sea to
heave her from her beach and drown her in its
pressure of black violence.

The monk and the nun were about her bed,
acutely directed on her, tuned to her every
manifestation. With eyes fast shut she lent
herself to their quiet directions, clinging to the
memory of her resolve that when the river
began to pull she would swim down with it,
clutching at no banks. With a touch of
anæsthetic from a gauze mask to help her she
went forward. Her mind went down and
lived in her body, ran out of her brain and
lived in her flesh. She had eyes and nose and
ears and senses in her body, in her backbone,
living like a spiny woodlouse, doubled in a

ball, having no beginning and no end. Now the first twisting spate of pain began. Swim then, swim with it for your life. If you resist, horror, and impediment! If you swim, not pain but sensation! Who knows the heart of pain, the silver, whistling hub of pain, the central bellows of childbirth which expels one being from another? None knows it who, in disbelief and dread has drawn back to the periphery, contradicting the will of pain, braking against inexorable movements. Keep abreast of it, rush together, you and the violence which is also you! Wild movements, hallucinated swimming! Other things exist than pain!

It is hard to gauge pain. By her movements, by her exclamations she would have struck horror into anyone but her monk and her nun. She would have seemed tortured, tossing, crying, muttering, grunting. She was not unconscious but she had left external life. She was blind and deaf to world surface. Every sense she had was down in Earth to which she belonged, fighting to maintain a hold on the pain, to keep pace with it, not to take an ounce of will from her assent to its passage. It was as though the dark river rushed her to a glossy arch. A little more, a little more, a little longer. She was not in torture, she was in labour; she had been thus before and knew her way. The corkscrew swirl swept her shuddering, until she swam into a tunnel—the first seconds of anæsthesia.

*   *   *   *

Now the shocked and vigorous cry of the born rang through the room. From its atavistic dim cradle, from a passage like death, crying with rage, resenting birth, came the freed and furious cave-child, coated in mystery, the heavy-headed, vulnerable young, the triumph of the animal world, the triumph of life.

Now out of her river the mother was drawn upwards, she became the welcomed, the applauded, the humoured. Faces smiled over her.

"What is it?" Nine months of wondering in one second solved.

"A boy, a beauty!"

("Doctors," said the mother, "say that! There are terrible things . . . that are not beauties.")

In a moment she had the creature laid into her arm, clad already in a woollen jersey and woollen leggings, the strange habits of man which it would wear to its death, now put on for the first time. Folded, and filled with a tiny flutter, its arms stirred, its fingers remained pointed, spatulate, a hand of stars. It had lately breathed. It was like death, this terrific and gay moment; she was solemn and light, weak, mystical and excited.

"Is it lunch-time?"

"Two o'clock."

"I'd like bread-and-milk and brown sugar."

Bread-and-milk and brown sugar were brought by magic. Idly she watched the gay activity in the room; the baby in his cot, warmed, over-warmed, like a child that has been fished out of the sea—the midwife folding garments. The doctor came in from the bath-room and pulled on his coat.

The squire tried to show her strength, to put herself back into life.

"Only two hours ago I was in the garden!"

"Keep quiet," said the doctor. "You look as though you were going to pop out of bed."

"She won't," said the midwife, tyranny in her eye.

"I'm frightfully excited, excited," complained the squire. "I want to talk, to brag. I'm twitching with excitement."

The doctor went to his bag and pulled out a hypodermic. "I'll give you a quarter of morphia," he said.

She held up her arm, and when the needle was withdrawn she waited, thinking of the baby. The curtains were pulled across the windows. Far away a telephone rang, but she listened more intently to the sleep that was drifting into her knees, creeping down from her knees to her ankles, stealing to her thighs, from her thighs to her heavy arms, and so it stole, hushing her body, member by member, into peace. Now only her head floated like a happy globe, staring at the pallor of the curtains. It was heaven to lie like this, she did not want to sleep, but sleep she did.

CHAPTER NINE

I T WAS SIX ON THE FOLLOWING MORNING.
The wood creaked, the handle turned,
there was a line of light under the bedroom
door. Softly the tall midwife in her dressing-gown, so unofficial, so intimate after
yesterday's battle, came through the door. The
mother drew sideways in her bed leaving room
beside her enough for a grown man, and the
midwife bent and laid the newborn in the valley.

"Have you slept well?" she asked the squire.

"Not stirred all night. And you?"

"Well enough."

(Who could sleep well, wardress of a first
night on earth, each breath of her charge
drawn with her knowledge, her approval, her
blessing on its strength and quality?)

"Look, he sucks!" The squire offered her
nipple to his mouth. Instantly the strange

action began. He showed now that he had but one fierce intention, to draw, to pull, to drag his way into life. Now that he was born all his life was in his mouth. He knew his job. While his lips worked his hands drifted out at angles, or hooked inwards with unconscious strength, the fingers first folded, or opened like a starfish; then one hand was wrung upon the other and both held forward like a supplication. Strange, slow, unchildish, womblike actions, while his new strong life was in his mouth. The midwife slipped away, having little brews to make; tea for the squire and for herself. The air was pouring through the windows, trees grew round, gold-sided brown birds ran up the sunshine on the roof and tugged and chattered at the corners of the tiles. The squire, bending over the baby, her watch in her hand, would have given him ten minutes, but he was so young he was not ripe for that.

At the end of five he drifted off the breast and sank to sleep. With shaking difficulty and hands unpractised since Henry she took him under his buttocks and heavy head and heaved him so that he lay flat upon her chest like a chrysalis, then shifting herself beneath him she put him into the warm ditch that she had left. He woke and tried the further breast, not drawing milk yet but an aperient, to cleanse his body from the vapours of birth.

Now he lay asleep, folded and severe, and she watched him, and in his sleep he waved his exquisite and unsteered hands, five-pointed and unspread. His face which had been flushed was now snow-white.

"So it was you!" said the squire to him, thinking of her nine months' companion, of her hardness towards him, now melted, of his quirks and movements to which she had grown so used, and thinking with wonderment, "So it was *you*."

The morphia still drifting about her like evaporating wool she lay in gentle happiness beside the baby, stroking the months that had passed, months swollen with a rising of the spirits like a bride's. How strangely the birth of a baby pressed away the menace of death

and assuaged in the breast that savage and
pitiful need for immortality!

Not for long would she possess the marvel of
the newly-born. Before it is tasted and spoken
of it is gone. Complete in itself it is never seen
again, and a child nursed and weaned is a child
with its spiritual navel-string cut; thereafter
the "mother" is but a woman loving her
young, her child already on its journey. But a
child in the womb or at the breast stops time.
Time stands still. Death recedes. All this she
knew.

Death recedes. Sick, growing, grumbling,
stumbling, happy, she had worked uphill for
months towards this end. Half-dazed, half-
mystic, she had felt the walls of her life stretch
and grow thin, the walls of her home, the
village, the gardens, the flowers in the border
flow into each other; had wandered about the
house, touching her children, talking to them,
released from life, released from time, released
from death. She had then no need to be quick
before eternity, she could not hurry. "You'll
be worse before you're better," said her father

in the ancient language of man towards birth.
Worse, but not worse off. It meant to her
"deeper in," up to the neck in it. It meant the
crash, the crisis, the strange day, the strange
midnight, the birthday,—and here she lay
washed up in the sunlight on this side of that
arch on her river.

The baby beside her slept with rising and
falling breast. Monstrous, staggering, she
thought, to plant a feeling heart in such a
bubble!

How her ambitions had changed! How
nature, almost without her consent, had set her
horizon on the next generation! How short a
time ago was it that she had cried, "*My* life!
My life!" stretching her arms and her young
body, fierce, alone, adventurous,—and now a
mother five times!

Life was no longer altogether hers, the body
already a little threadbare, worn in indescribable
yet noted ways. Since these essential acts of
birth had occurred she knew that there was
something in which she now acquiesced, a
calm, a stoic pleasure in *procession*. "To give

birth, to bring up the young, to die" thought the squire, and for the first time saw her own end as endurable. "I was solid and I was myself. But now I am a pipe through which the generations pass."

*　　*　　*　　*

After the ten o'clock breast-feed, which was no breast-feed yet but a rehearsal, the squire asked for the children. The midwife replied indifferently that they were "about."

The squire insisted. "But I want them!"

The midwife was tired. Her work now was harder than the squire's, she had still a thousand things to do.

"But I want them!" pleaded the squire. "I must keep him here in my bed till they have seen him."

"It would be better if he came away with me now," said the midwife. "They can see him to-morrow."

The squire looked as though she might cry, wanting her own way.

The midwife, not astonished, went to fetch

the children. Lucy and Jay came in and stood beside the bed.

"Don't poke him," said the squire.

"Boniface won't come," said Jay.

"Not to see *me?*" said the squire.

Outside the door the midwife was arguing in a low tone.

"I don't care to," said Boniface's firm voice. The midwife murmured.

"I don't care to see it," said Boniface.

"Boniface won't come in," said the midwife entering, "but here's Henry."

"Here's me," said Henry and walked across to the bed. He looked long and earnestly at the baby. Jay had finished looking already, and was at the dressing-table, fiddling.

"Leave my hair-spray alone," said the squire, already tired and testy.

Henry still looked at the baby, his conqueror, the enemy of his babyhood.

"Boniface should be made to come," murmured the squire, wanting him.

"Why should I?" said Boniface's voice, he listening outside the door.

The squire altered her tone and put an edge on it. "Come in at once!"

At that he came, reassured, his shirt hanging out in front, his fly-buttons undone, his lower lip covered with toothpaste.

"Here it is," said the squire, showing him the baby.

"H'm," he said, and put his hands in his pockets.

Now she had them all together, and the midwife was growing restive. Henry's interest too had evaporated; all four roved about the room.

"Can I light matches?" said Henry, dismissing the birth.

"They must all go," said the midwife. Lucy glared.

"Let Lucy stay a minute," said the squire. Lucy smiled.

The boys went out of the room, but Boniface turned, smiled at his mother through his hanging, uncombed hair, and said with something sweet and awake in his face——

"Good-bye."

157

The squire lay still after Lucy, and the baby too, had gone, thinking bridal thoughts. The baby and herself, two. Those two. The baby and herself. How important to be alone, how vital to be alone. When would the milk come in? She heard Pratt's footfall, unmistakably his, regal, pounding, unhurried, pass her door and his tap fall on the midwife's adjoining room. Bunches of flowers from Caroline, and could she see her for a second?

"Not a second! Not a second!" scribbled the squire. "I too am in love. But go and have a happy meeting at the boat."

She imagined the lit sea through which the boat must ride, as Caroline shaded her eyes. Caroline on the quayside in one of her dresses, so slim, so moulded, Caroline showing him the other house, the ilex trees, the garden, cocktails laid out, gay chairs, luncheon in the open-doored room, the drift of the afternoon (what would she do with him?) changing for dinner, candlelight. But if Caroline took him in her arms he would never be small and hers like the baby. You could not get under the flesh of another, you could not fold him and hold him in the hollow of breasts, warm like a living doll but with the sleeping mind of man under the domed skull. What was Caroline really going to do to-night, that perpetual happy victim of attack?

In all relationships that she had hitherto known, in childhood, in friendship, in love, in mating, the partner fought, the partner struggled to live, to command, to break away, or to break in. But here for a short while she held in her arms the perfect companion, fished out of her body and her nature, coming to her for sustenance, falling asleep five times a day in her arms, exposing its greed, its inattention, its pleasure and its peace, going red with anger in her arms, and white with digesting sleep.

And Caroline, what had she got? (But it depends what you want, said the squire.) Exquisite young man, full of enemy and conspiring thoughts, moving always towards or away, but still never. Attacking, attacking, or in flight. Restless, needing to culminate. So you grew through men into this motherhood, wanting, wanting, with a fierce longing to see the children grow.

She heard the baby cry angrily, a new note and a new tone, not heard since Henry. The cry came out in a curve like a cat's claw. It seemed to scratch the air. Reaow . . . reaow . . . She cared not a rap, knowing whose hands tended him and that he was too lately born to be hungry. Milk would come in soon, to-night perhaps or to-morrow morning. Meanwhile he must cry and free his lungs and take exercise. Soon the noise stopped. She imagined how he had flung his arms above his head, how he slept. She moved in the bed in a new comfort, slim and hollowed, looking forward to her doctor, who would come in, fresh and caustic, gay as a husband over his "birth."

Nurse came in, beaming, carrying six carnations she had bought in the village. "He's lovely," breathed Nurse, "Oh, he's lovely!" She could hardly wait till the month was up and she took him over. And, never understanding at each successive birth her lady's sound and hearty condition, she took to whispering. But the midwife was at the door beckoning; afraid that Nurse would tell the squire that Mrs. Lynch had not appeared that morning in the kitchen. Nurse, burning to say it, had refrained. There were rumours all over the house that Mrs. Lynch was in her bedroom but had not slept it off. She and Mr. Lynch had had a party to celebrate the birth. Nothing of this must set the squire's mind aching with the old sore "servants . . . servants" before the milk came in.

"They ought to be out of their households," thought the midwife (thinking of "mothers"). And the old dream came over her of the "palisading." A nunnery-clinic where mothers could be set apart from the world, for more than a month, for two, for three, so that lazily and fully, like cattle, they could feed their young.

Beneath and around the squire the household was seething, Pratt withdrawn, revolted, remembering his axiom that it was salvation to let things slide, kept his eyes shut and himself in the pantry.

Mrs. Lynch had been singing in her bed-room half the night and she had taken Mr. Lynch to bed with her. Mr. Lynch had now come down and was sitting on the kitchen chair without his boots. He looked shaken. Ruby and Queenie giggled in the servants' hall, but Ruby, on whom the work would fall, was growing indignant. The nurserymaid had told it all to Nurse, and Nurse had told the midwife. The midwife, tucking the baby into his cot with a deft hand, tight, tight that he might not miss the womb, resolved to send for Pratt.

Pratt, coming upstairs, walked first to the sleeping baby on the balcony, and as he looked at it there was tenderness on his dark face. Something in his dulled and tired ferocity was stirred at the sight of the newborn. All the two hundred and more nights that he had waited at dinner on the growing squire had come to this. Often in his grave way he had looked at her, and now here lay the child. This is what he would have liked himself, a

boy of his own. The women he couldn't
endure, but a child, a boy of his own, that was
what he had missed out of life. He turned to
listen to what the midwife had to say.

Where, in the wrappings of inherited
servitude, lay the truth in Pratt? Was it his
creed or his cowardice that dictated his refusal
to thrust Mrs. Lynch and her mate from the
house? Stubbornly he told the midwife that
what she asked was difficult for him. He
recognised her strength. But not till he was in
the last ditch would he take over unpleasant
command. Live and let live. Life was bleak
and cooks his enemies, but the pantry was his
chapel and he could hitch it round him like a
garment and curse all intruders. At his refusal
the midwife, her face taut, went downstairs.
Pratt, as he left the room, cast a look back at
the baby. He was not weak or tender, but
violently he wanted a son.

Ruby hung near the kitchen door but was
sent out. The midwife found Mrs. Lynch
attending to her dishes. Mr. Lynch sat nursing
his weak stomach in the window chair.

"I must speak to you," said the midwife, starched and very tall, her newborn threatened. Mrs. Lynch held up her slanting face.

"You must leave, Mrs. Lynch," said the midwife, without preamble.

"And why?" said Mrs. Lynch, her face evil and still but her hands shaking.

"Why?" said the midwife, her voice low and sharp with anger. "Because what you do threatens my work. A baby has been born in this house. If you cannot understand what that means you must go."

"And if I don't! Suppose I won't! Who are you to give orders?"

"I am medically in charge here. If you don't go upstairs now and pack your case and leave I must telephone for the doctor."

"Johnny," said Mrs. Lynch, "d'you hear her!" But Johnny never moved a muscle. "I wouldn't stay a minute," shouted Mrs. Lynch, "where I wasn't wanted!" and picking up a large china dish she broke it on the corner of the table.

"Keep down yor stinking temper,"

said Johnny very suddenly to the floor.

"So that's it is it!" said Mrs. Lynch, and with an exclamation she caught him on the side of the cheek. Almost in one movement he put her flat upon the floor. Making past her, dangling his boots in his hands, he went out. The midwife turned, and calling Pratt from the pantry, she thrust him into action.

"You must see to *this*," she said, pointing to the kitchen. "There is nothing owing, and the woman must be out of the house in half an hour." Pratt went into the kitchen and shut the door.

"Where is the kitchenmaid?" said the midwife. Ruby crept out of the servants' hall, her eyes shining.

"I'm sure you can cook?" said the midwife with heightened colour.

"Yes, some things," said Ruby.

"You must carry on for a day or two," said the midwife. "Would you like to come upstairs with me?"

She showed Ruby the baby in his cot, and talked to her quietly of his mother, of the milk, of the necessity for peace, of Ruby's own share in the business of peace. Ruby did not listen to much of it, but she bent over the baby with her thick young animal face alight.

CHAPTER TEN

IN TWO DAYS THE MIDWIFE HAD INSTALLED
a woman in the kitchen whom the squire
would never have had the luck to choose.
She told the squire of it in the sunny afternoon,
well between breast-feeds. The milk had come
in and the baby fed quietly and with strength.

"What's her name, the cook? I don't even
know her name!"

"Mrs. Limit's her name. She's quiet and
Scotch and knows her work. Ruby has settled
down quite well with her."

"Oh . . ." cried the squire, "stay for ever
and protect me! Never go!"

"Ah, no! It's only around a birth that I can
try to make people do well. They'll do something for a baby."

"Mrs. Lynch didn't."

"She was a terrible woman," said the

midwife. "How could you possibly have taken her?"

"What is one to do at these interviews?" said the squire. "A woman offers herself, wearing some strange mask which she keeps on for a while. One has twenty minutes to decide and few alternatives. I thought her cold, still look, meant efficiency. I thought her icy eye meant she could manage the kitchenmaid. She was neat. She carried a little case. She looked like a secretary."

"You should get them when they look like cooks," said the midwife mildly.

The baby was four days old. Now he would come in in the dawn, regally in the midwife's arms, already expectant. He fed greedily at one breast, and as his mother passed him over her body in the darkness to the other he snuffled in a passion of impatience, learning already that there was a second meal, seizing the nipple, choking, and sinking to hard-working silence. Sensory exploration which, in the peril of his first day on earth, had centred only in his lips, now spread to his limbs, and

his hand, as he worked, from lying stiff like a
star, began to move, travelling over the
squire's silk nightdress, scratching the silk
with his nail in a flurry of his finger, trying the
linen sheet, learning the textures. Flinging his
hand with a sudden movement behind his head
he hit the silver travelling clock. Instantly in
the half-light a look of interest broke into his
eyes. Letting go, half-turning his head—
"What, what?" his marmoset eyes demanded.
But the moment of concentration over he
went back to his life's work. All his power
was in his lips. His hands were fronds,
convolvulus-tendrils, catching at surfaces, but
only half-informed.

Watching the squire, piercingly sleepless,
he would be asleep in a moment.

When he had ridden away and been tucked
down, the squire and the midwife talked about
him, two women in love; but during the
breast-feeds the midwife withdrew, leaving the
squire alone to let down her milk.

Strange, concentrated life, that no man
knows, shared with the cat in the stable and

the bitch in the straw of the kennel, but lit
with the questions of the marvelling human
brain. The regularity of her milk, as always,
astonished the squire. At six and ten and two
and six and ten, to the tick, to the instant, her
breasts swelled and reminded her. A moment
later she heard the midwife's hand on the
door. Even in the dawn she woke punctually,
or her breasts woke her. "Taken over, bag
and baggage, for him," she thought. "Com-
plex, civilized being that I am, I am turned into
an hour-glass." The baby too moved through
his ritual, punctual as a clock. And behind
both of them watched the midwife, keeping
mother and child on the rails of development
with fine movements, setting order into the
baby's life, creating peace, keeping off the
world, watching, reflecting, adjusting, jockey-
ing the untidiness of civilization into perfection, teaching even so tiny a baby manners
and endurance; to cry at the proper time for
exercise, to sleep at the proper hour. She was
a virgin with a clock, she was a God-virgin to
him, serving him with sweetness, severity,

evenness and calm, wondering sometimes as she thought of all her "mothers" why so much stress was laid upon physical maternity.

"Is there a bond between him and me besides the milk?" asked the squire wonderingly as she looked down at the gorged and sleeping baby, growing whiter with the pallor of digestion.

"Is there?" said the midwife, cupping her chin in her fine hand. "There must be," said the squire. "Think of the last months!" But the midwife was thinking of so many spoilt, lax mothers, slovenly, forced into their maternity, of bursts of animal affection and pride, of ignorant or vain or lovely women, who because they were "mothers" assumed that all was well. Behind her, into the Middle Ages and far behind that, stretched the medieval line of priestesses, wise-women, gamps, midwives, threading their way slowly up to the fine instrument which she had become.

"There *is*," she said at last, so long after that the squire had forgotten her question.

"There *is* something between a mother and her baby, other than the appeasing of its desire. 'Mothering,' the doctors called it in the children's hospital. The babies do well with the mother."

"Is that odd?"

The grave blue eyes turned towards her, charged with their measured look.

"I have in my time," said the midwife, "questioned the value of motherhood. I have seen so many bad mothers, poor, indifferent mothers. Yet often the babies do well with them. Often, when I have left a mother, the baby has prospered without me; though the mother was terrified at being left, and the milk gone down with her anxiety at my departure. There *is* something between the mother and the baby. Not only love, not only milk. Some sort of closeness. A baby when it has been so close to her needs to be close again after it is born. My position towards them together should be that of a hand-maiden. I clean the dishes, I lay the table, I *serve* the mother with the child!"

She who had known how to be obedient to her training, now knew with a sure touch how to take up the reins herself. Twenty years of observation she had had, drawing babies out of mystery into life, setting them on their path, leaving a standard behind her in house after house, dropping here and there a word to the nurses she left behind her, to the girls who "took over," hardening her heart to leave the baby she had held in the cup of her care to rougher usage. Infinite, forestalling care she tried to teach them while the creature lay heavy-headed and naked to injury under her reign. And soon, so soon, when her quick eye knew that the baby had put on a garment of invisible strength, she would set her thoughts towards other, unborn babies, growing restless, making ready for departure. And this had something about it of the heart-carelessness of Death. Only Death and a midwife can so pass on from love to love.

There was much to do in these first few days, but time for talk, too. They talked of the doctor, their daily visitor.

"And what a profession!" ended the squire. "And what a priesthood! Don't tell me that a doctor is like the rest of us! By the pressure of his extraordinary training, by the position towards us he occupies he is forever changed, he is for ever a little like God. There's something left on earth, very salty, when you face those experienced eyes and struggle with speech. When, half-articulate, scared, talkative, exposed, you find that you are denied your private life, and that your talk is being selected or discarded on lines to which you have no clue. Have you, serving your priests, ever regretted your profession?"

"There comes a moment," said the midwife hesitatingly, "there come moments when a nurse who really cares for her work knows that she must abandon life; a long and haunting period when the woman in the nurse is still conscience-stricken about the farewell to sex."

"Men," said the squire, "encourage that haunting. It is a life-instinct in them which says, 'Not a woman must be lost to us, lest she be that spot of soil in which to fertilize

the superman!' You're a drone; a grand, a
gallant, a formidable and nearly divine drone.
You and those like you have become a third
sex. But the trouble is that men won't let a
woman be a drone with honour!"

"I must go," said the midwife rising. "I
must get him ready for his feed. And you are
getting tired and excited just when you should
not."

"Ah, no!" said the squire. "Tired? I love
to talk! I, too, am saying the farewell to sex.
I, too, am looking to a future in which I shall
find again what life is made of, bare life,
without mirage, without props. . . ." So
after the talks founded on *their* years of living,
in *he* rode, the rapidly-growing shoot of life,
the little child with his crooked, hooked arms
and his embryonic actions, pressing forward to
his work, starting in with fury and wearing a
kitten's look as he slept off. So he was brought
to his mother at all kinds and colours of hours,
breaking the flow of her thoughts and her talk
into sections, at the hour of dusk, the hour of
dawn, the hour of artificial lights, the midday

hour, so developed this marvellous flirtation, this appeasing of one wild desire. She had not yet begun to read over his head and shut him out with books as soon she would do, but hung over him raised on her elbow in the bed watching his spine of thin gold hair, his perpetual movements, his hands curving inward to the thumb. And he watched her as he suckled with his blue bird's eye (she hardly knowing what he saw), watched her as though he read everything in the nod and shadow of her head above him. But it was an absent stare, and with a quiver the blond lashes dropped and he was blotted out. Blotted out like a gassed child, and so lay, his fingers petrified, sticking up at angles. She watched him, thinking and dreaming, feeling life short, shiveringly short. And the bubble of wind within him forcing its way upward as from a vase that has been too hastily filled, he would stir and snuffle, give a wandering pipe, open his eyes, while his face slowly flushed in anger and he prepared for his cry. Then the squire, growing stronger, with the definite hands of a

well-accustomed mother, would lift him over
her shoulder and pop his wind for him, the
little bubble that had disturbed him coming up
like a naughty spirit, and his head hanging
helplessly goggling and staring with surprise
over her shoulder, till such time as she laid
him down for his final sleep and he was
carried away.

*   *   *   *

Gentle life, with the little untroublesome
companion. Any trouble was the midwife's;
all the heaven was the squire's.

CHAPTER ELEVEN

IT WAS INCOMMUNICABLE TO CAROLINE, and nearly to the midwife, what the mother got out of watching the children. While they seemed young to her they seemed of pressing, of oncoming importance. As horses in the distance are seen small yet she knew the wind of their hooves, she felt the beating ground as they came towards her. To Caroline they were of static youth, aged four, and so and so and so, but to their mother they were passing like explorers through virgin country, their hands on the door-handle of the future. Their personalities as they swelled seemed to attract new particles from some unseen contemporary mine, as though there lodged a magnet in the children's minds.

The midwife was too specialized upon the very young really to care to understand. Life was too vast, too complicated, too full of the implications of growth, for it to be possible to observe more than a corner. To snatch the newborn from the inchoate, to set it on its feet, to get the milk going, the standard in the household fixed, to hold this nebulous moment like a witch's ball glittering with to-morrow, took all the midwife's breath. These other growing children, thickened over with flesh, wilful, impeding, belonged to a different section of time and to other specialists. So she listened to tales of them with an abstracted air, and a feeling that no part of her mother's attention should be taken from the baby. Each child had been the midwife's special charge at one moment; she had borned them all. But what she had cared for in each, bending over it, had been so near the egg. These great birds, kicking and flying, ruffled her with the wind of their passing. Even Henry.

So, in the spring mornings, with the small spring fire burning behind its tall guard, she brought the newly born in to bath before his

mother, to decoy her, to fluff up her motherhood, to bring the milk down. It was part of a
design. For the only thing the midwife
fought in the squire was the running, plunging
mind of the mature woman, which would not
stay low and warm beside its baby.

Sometimes the squire still held him in her
spirit like a daffodil bulb held in the earth; but
now she was beginning to stare out over his
head, to fret for her knit family, to ask for the
bustle and the contact back in her life. With
the flow of the milk not perfectly established
she would let fall the pile of newspapers and
books beside her bed and, just before a breast-
feed, plunge excitedly into debate with herself,
with the midwife, set flying the wheels in her
restless brain, checking the mysterious flow
of the milk. She would lean over the baby
impatiently, watching the hands of the clock;
and the midwife, returning later with the baby
from the weighing machine, would say re-
proachfully, "Two ounces short."

"But I will try again!" the squire cried,
holding out her arms. And the midwife,

shaking her head, carried the baby into the garden.

"You should be *alone*," she said suddenly, one evening when they had finished dinner.

The squire, starting, looked at her, then remembered the morning's trouble. She felt vexed, and grew restless. The instrument of her household had so many keys; she longed to be back at her playing. Boniface's abstractions, Henry's cool looks, Jay's gaiety like a yelping terrier, Lucy's pother with the lot. That was her full, struck chord, and the new note, white and voiceless, ready to be inserted.

Yet this baby, what heaven, what a drug, to lie back with it, play with it, lean over its unfolding, live its cosy life! And this is what she should have done, what the midwife longed for her to do, what would have calmed child and mother and fed the child in some strange and perfect manner unconnected with ounces. But because life was blazing outside her room, because voices clutched at her through the walls, because the "palisading" was not there and there was no nunnery to enclose her with her young, she started up, and looked impatiently towards her boundaries.

"I should be alone," she agreed, lying back again in the bed. "But being here I am what I am. I cannot abdicate. We have to make compromises. What do you believe?"

"I should be nearer-sighted," said the midwife. "I have to pore over the beginnings. I believe that all is done in these first few weeks. It is not my job to look beyond these days, for this present is my work. But if you ask me to look, and to speak of what I can't really know, I should say that as your baby is now so he will be in old age, that the perfection of his introduction to life will reassert itself again and again in all his crises, and in that greatest of all crisis the slow sinking of the body into age."

The squire looked at her. "How you care!" she said.

"I care so much," said the midwife, sitting straighter, "that I am prepared to give up the baby—the victim of centuries of women—to the attack of man!"

The squire's eyes opened.

"The book of instinct has long, long been closed," said the midwife.

"But what do we get instead?" said the squire. "The science-guided baby! Labelled, its tears and stools in bottles, its measurements on a chart, its food weighed like a prescription!"

"Better than muddle," said the midwife.

Pratt came up to announce Caroline. The midwife left them alone.

"What does one feel," said Caroline ardently, forgetful of the birth, bringing the breath of her new adventure into the room and sitting with it under the squire's nose. "What does one feel, when one meets a man one has once loved?"

"Nothing!" said the squire, straight out from her bed.

"What?" (startled) "don't be ridiculous! Do you mean that there ever can be 'nothing' left? After such intimacy?"

"Nothing at all," said the squire, instantly ready to talk. "Boredom. If ever there was a cup that was empty that one is! If there was love, without hindrance, and it's gone . . . it's gone because it's burnt out, finished. Nothing more boring than for the protagonists to meet. They've said everything, done everything, explored every corner and left the country! They don't want to camp there again."

(Shocked). "But isn't there a tenderness?"

"No," said the squire. "Not till one is old and there is nothing to hope. There can't be tenderness when it's an aggravation to meet. It's always an aggravation for a woman to meet a man from whom she is sure she can expect nothing, to whom she is no mystery, who knew her so well and yet could fall apart from her. The tenderness could only reinstate itself in old age, or because nothing ever really happened between them."

"Ah . . . I don't know."

"Nothing so boring!" insisted the talkative squire. "I'm never so bored. The poor old conversation, pegs lower than it used to be, opaque, without mystery. It's not natural to

be a monument to memory. I forget everything. When he comes I hope he'll go
soon."

"Who?"

"Any him, who was once godalmighty. If
he comes at all he generally comes in the
children's hour!"

"You're hopeless! You deserve that that
nursery should grow up and forget you!
You sacrifice everything to it, all your
friends."

"If there's one thing certain," said the squire
more slowly, "it is that my friends will let me
down. When they crouch in by their fires in
old age it will be by their own fires, not mine.
There's a chance the children will come sometimes and watch me crouch at mine. 'Sacrifice!'
The children are more *fun* than my contemporaries! Look what strangers we all are!
Look how you will drop me at the call of a
telephone! Look how we say the same thing,
the same thing, the same things! And look
what the children say! Something that comes
out of a new heart, not a strained mind. They

grow, they move, and the world is to be theirs. But whom have you met? What love-peg, trailing his glory in his hand like a dressing gown behind him?"

Caroline spoke then of her long-past, first, astonishing, and nearly calamitous love.

"He came down? When?"

"Yesterday. For lunch."

"You surprise me! What age did he look?"

"It's true—a bit dyed . . . but very vital. He must be sixty-four now, ferocious as ever, truculent, roaring, very noisy but very fine."

"Did you feel proud of your first love affair?"

"I hadn't a chance against him," said Caroline. "His fame, the glory of his talk, the way he rushed me! These broke down my upbringing. I did love him. I loved him."

"And what did you feel yesterday?"

There was a long pause. "Awkward," said Caroline at last.

"Awkward . . ." murmured the squire. "An awkward horse, difficult to sit on. An awkward situation, difficult to sit on, and wished well over. 'Awkward' is a good word, not condemning, nobody's fault, an act of God which must be borne and then forgotten."

"Yes. Like that," said Caroline.

"And what about this tenderness you were upholding?"

"He talked of that."

"My *dear* Caroline! Look it full in the face It's like the bathroom steam, wet and evaporating. *He* talked of it! He's old now. He goes about gathering up the women who loved him and getting a kick out of their consternation and vague distress. He whips up what they once felt and hopes to make it foam. He tries his foot on his own immortality and there the ice is thin and lets him through. I'm boiling with metaphors. Don't you be disturbed, darling, by your old jackanapes!"

"When I think——"

"——don't think! You wouldn't think if he hadn't come. Never look at old photographs. The dead, *dear* Caroline, are meant to fade. From the moment of death they begin to

recede. Even the beloved dead recede. When
they do not it is because something abnormal
has happened to the soul. You are a woman
meant to walk from man to man and never to
look back. It will pass, and perhaps you and
I will have our old age together, the one grown
more like the other—in the end. But don't
let's have any nonsense on the path. Why,
memory! There is nothing so difficult to
remember as sexual love. How often, where,
and what happened? It all goes, it has all gone,
leaving no impression, mattering so much less
than we like to think."

"But something remains."

"You cling to this idea that 'something
remains'. What we have had we have had,
and, pleased, we pass along. (But what we
haven't had may well be a ticklish business!)
And what's the good of my talking! You
haven't got where I have, you are not as old
and as plain and as satisfied. And indeed I
very often live again in you!"

The midwife came in.

"Oh!" said Caroline rising. And then in

horror, "I haven't seen the baby! That's what I came for!"

The squire snorted and laughed.

"Can she see the baby?"

"He is coming up for his feed," said the midwife. "Better not."

"You're angry," said Caroline, pleading, "because I forgot him. And I came on purpose to see him! To see what I had missed."

The midwife understood her perfectly, but without sympathy.

"Better leave it now," she said, withdrawn. "—Another time."

"Come on Sunday," said the squire. But Caroline fled, waving good nights, to her own house behind the ilexes.

"You're an iron woman," said the squire, flat on her back, after a while. "When you keep her out you keep my youth away."

The midwife looked troubled and paused in the doorway pondering.

"I felt an atmosphere," she said at length, softly, "that wasn't right for so young a baby."

"Psychic?" said the squire. "Even after all

189

the science and pressure of your training?"

"You are not pleased," said the midwife, still hesitant and troubled.

"No," said the squire. "No. That lovely creature is my youth!"

"But in your youth you did not want this baby."

"Nothing that I have ever been could do him damage. That is life."

"He is eight days old," said the midwife. "So young. He is my charge, and my judgment must hold sway. I am virginal and narrow, but I am his gardener. You will soon have him."

"Can such a thing be?"

"What?"

"That a woman, leaning over a baby, can shed an influence?"

"Eight days," said the midwife, and in her face was the look which made her all she was. "Who knows?" She left the room to fetch the baby.

*   *   *   *

On Sunday it was raining faintly. Sunday

in summer, raining softly as the congregation came at midday from the church gate. The squire's bed was in the window that over-looked the Green and the church, and Caroline looked out with her.

"Are those indeed women?" said Caroline, nodding to the Green.

"Who?" said the squire, thinking of something else. Then following Caroline's gaze she saw four women in mackintoshes, conferring together, pointing to the War Memorial.

"They're not delicious harlots, if that's what you mean."

"That's really what I meant," said Caroline, smiling.

"You're quite right," said the squire. "Such as *you* ought to be called 'women'. *We* ought to be called 'wumen'; some different word. Wumen are hard-working, faulty, honest, female males—trudging down life, pushing the future before them in a wheelbarrow. Wumen are petty labourers; with handicaps."

"Are you blackening me?" said Caroline.

"No. You're the thing that man sees when

191

he says 'woman'. You spend time on it, you spend your life on it. Sex, like poetry, lives longer in a nature that has time for it, time to listen, time to keep still. The very tendrils of the body need silence to thrum. Why else are beds and darkness such good soil?"

The wet green trees warbled with birds. "It's exquisite," said Caroline, thinking, as always, of herself, "and yet indeed it's always the same thing over again, and what do I get out of it?"

"Yes, what do you?"

"I'm a complaisant victim," said Caroline. "Something like that. To be asked is heaven. To consent is heaven. But to give is . . . what I pay."

"If you said that to a man he would say you had no temperament."

"They say that," said Caroline. "So then I never tell them the truth."

"Man," said the squire, "honest man, busy like a boy on life . . . he longs for us to share what he has. So we soothe his brow, and tell him all is well."

"And all *is* well," said Caroline. "But unexplainably."

The midwife stirred in the next room, the door alightly ajar.

"Hush," said the squire. "If we must talk of women, talk quietly. These problems distress her."

"But they are problems of that earth which brings forth her seeds!"

The squire did not go on talking. The midwife and Caroline were too far apart, the midwife too strange, too flaming an ally to be caught for Caroline to look at—who would listen but would not understand.

What the squire thought, what she did not say to Caroline, was that Caroline's future was in danger, not yet, but some day—that complaisant victim who could not live without her attackers.

Caroline too had these wild fears in bed that night behind the ilex trees. She resolved that next morning she would go to Venice.

*   *   *   *

When the midwife had folded her up for the night, lights out, windows adjusted, the squire after a wrestle with the spirited darkness put on the light and sat up in bed to lean her head in her hands.

She shook herself, hearing that bay of distress that comes in the night like the cry of an animal in a deep wood, that comes out of the soul.

"What am I?" she whispered into her hands, unable to sleep. "My excitement, imagination, vitality, gift for life—are like a spray that falls again on to the ground and is lost and sopped up. I am lost every day. By every nightfall all is lost."

She pulled, for distraction, a volume of Montaigne's *Essays* from the shelf above her head. So new a friend was he, however, that many of the pages in the fat, white-bound edition were uncut, and she slipped the silver page-cutter out of her spectacle case. The figure of the giver of the cutter stood a moment by her bed and she paused to think of him. "When it isn't fun any more," she had said

to Caroline, "we must beat it," or words to
that effect. And the silver paper-cutter was
left over—a useful little object. "If I had been
capable," she said to the ghost, "of giving you
more I might have saved something beyond
this. But time presses, and I haven't the
strength to be burdened with worn loves. It's
true some women put up with the leaf-lace
pressed between pages and sniff the hardly-
evocative smell. But I must have actualities!
Living love around me like a growth!" In the
light turned on by her bed she saw her own
face in the glass on the wall opposite, the face
of a vigorous creature growing tired very
slowly in the service of life. She stared at its
heavier lines with her still young eyes. "It
won't catch them any more," she said, and
looked more intently. Resolute, heavy face.
All the tough honesty of early childhood had
returned again, and the fires and beauties of
girlhood that had taken her such strange
voyages had passed out as a mirage goes off
the horizon, leaving the country truly mapped
and exact.

She turned to Montaigne and opening him at random she read,—"God is favourable to those whom He makes to die by degrees; 'tis the only benefit of old age; the last death will be so much less painful; it will kill but a half or a quarter of a man. There is one tooth lately fallen out without drawing and without pain; it was the natural term of its duration; in that part of my being several others are already dead, others half dead, of those that were most active and in the first rank during my vigorous years; 'tis so I melt and steal away from myself."

And further,—"I have portraits of myself taken at five-and-twenty and five-and-thirty years of age. I compare them with that lately drawn; how many times is it no longer me; how much more is my present image unlike the former, than unlike my dying one?"

Without regret or fear the squire contemplated the page, and hearkened over four centuries to the voice of commonsense and courage. "It is only now that I start on my middle journey," she thought. "Long and

magnificent, and in great stages, life goes by."
Laying down the book she fell at once asleep,
appeased by company.

At dawn, again, with the birds gabbling, she
received her child. The pigeons were scramb-
ling in the trees, gross birds pretending to be
wild. Every now and then they alit on spring
boughs with the noise of elephants at leisure.
In came the little child in the fog of his babyhood, his eyes bright, his perception dim, and
was laid beside the figure that had so lately
been his casket. Now already as he sucked his
eyes rolled in curiosity, so that the whites
shone. Now already his bent arms moved over
the sheet and the fingers plucked and dis-
covered, and sometimes when he received
messages through a finger he would strain
round, dropping the nipple.

Then catching hold again in a second's
frenzy of loss this marvellous and manly doll
drew sternly at his mother's breast, a slight
frown on his new brow, the slight fleece
gleaming on his cranium. His unused hands
waved, grasping and loosing without purpose

or skill—hands that would later distinguish him from the animal world, lover's hands, father's hands, hands with an index finger, the little key to the door of life—waving slower and slower as he came to the close of his meal and slept, his nose bent by the weight of the breast.

CHAPTER TWELVE

THE SQUIRE PUT ON A LOOSE DRESS AND stood upright. She now knew that the room was smaller than for days she had supposed, that the spaces in it could be crossed. It was no longer her home. She sat that evening for the first time in the library with the children around her. To Boniface she said, "Have you missed me?"

"No I've been happy," he replied.

Lucy giggled. Taken aback the squire murmured,

"Then you were happy?"

"A little less——" mumbled Boniface, waving his arm.

Henry, trying to put Boniface in the wrong, said seriously, "*I've* missed you," but no one took any notice. Jay was gallant, with a bunch of flowers, Lucy ready to be up in arms should there be any sentiment.

But there was none. The squire was chuckling in her heart contentedly. She had got them all again, and she had done a fresh sum and made them five—good, sound work, and if she had had to be absent a little and loosen her hold and was playing them rustily, never mind. They did not know yet that they were part of her flesh, her past, her heredity, her mother and her father, they did not know till they grew older that they could barely escape her and what she brought down to them. Yet each had a chance of escape, each had a chance of being, not a grandchild, but a grandfather. In every family there is the seed of a new start, something transcending the family mixture, an explosion, a creation, and the Phœnix is born. Out of this the squire hoped for immortality.

"What is the smell in the room?" she said sniffing.

"Manure," said Lucy, without looking up. "On my shoes."

"You're supposed to keep your stable ones in the harness-room."

"I mixed them up. Both pairs are stable ones since you've been ill."

"Keying up!" said the squire. "There'll be a lot of keying up."

"Yes," said Jay, "Henry wants keying up."

"Wants what?" said Henry.

"You've got spoilt," said Jay calmly.

"*You're* spoilt," said Henry nimbly, looking black.

As like as two peas, and out for trouble, the baby with no conception that he was unarmed.

"He's been showing off," said Lucy into the page of her book. "He lay down on his back in a shop yesterday."

"I lay down on my back," said Henry.

"Why did you lie on your back?"

"I lay down on my back!" said Henry, jumping up and down on the sofa.

"Stop that! You'll burst the springs."

"Where are the springs?"

"Why did you lie down on your back?"

"Idiotic," said Lucy, reading. "Perfectly idiotic."

"Don't do it again, Henry," said the squire

201

sharply, speaking into the nape of Henry's neck. His whitish hair swept the floor as he hung on his stomach from the seat of the sofa upside down.

"Would the springs burst?" he murmured. "There's three dominoes under here."

"Then they've never moved the sofa!" said the squire to herself. "Dusting . . . keying up . . . never moved the sofa . . ." She grew a little hot from weakness, and glanced at the clock. The midwife came in to turn the children out of the room before the six o'clock breast-feed. They went with grumbles and cross looks. "That cursed baby!" muttered Jay in the doorway. "Ho!" said Boniface, struck by this, and stood still, his red face pleased and alive. But Lucy pulled him away through the doorway.

"When can they stay during the feeds?" asked the squire.

"Oh, not yet, not yet!" said the midwife, a little out of breath. "If the milk were properly established I would not be here!"

Now that the squire had the freedom of the

house the house also had the freedom of the
squire. Queenie was sick of Pratt. She said
so, and gave in her notice. Questioned, Pratt
appeared surprised and gloomy. "The girl is
frivolous," was all he would say. The squire
raged at his studied limpness. He who was
strong as iron simply lifted his hands from the
machine. He behaved as if he had no hope in
its ultimate smooth-running and no interest
in himself as its mechanic. And indeed he had
neither. Being beyond hope or pleasure he
was sunk in his subterranean world of dis-
illusion and self-repression. But ill-tempered,
and perhaps even ill-natured, he had virtues
that caused him discomfort, prides, clarity of
mind, occasional strange recognition of natural
beauty, an awakening of half-willing interest
when he heard the squire talk at dinner.

"Won't you pull harder with me?" the
squire had once asked of him. "We could
keep this household, between us, together;"
and never had she been so conscious of his
spiritual recoil, of his sullen stand before his
liberty, that liberty of which he made no use.

"The girl is frivolous," said Pratt.

"No use persuading her to stay then?"

"It is as your ladyship wishes."

"But can you get another?"

Pratt produced a deep and complicated murmur which contained neither an assent nor a negative. He was a master of this peculiar noise. He knew if he leant back and did nothing the squire would get a girl. The squire knew it too and cursed him impatiently in her soul. Often she said to herself that the twelve-year reign of Pratt was the reason for twelve years of staff difficulties, but she could not contemplate tearing him up. It was almost a friendship. For while she could feel the storm blowing behind his implacable frontage she was drawn too by his recognition of herself as the enemy-friend.

He was not against her, he would only circumvent her. He would allow her to take no step into the country of despair that he had mapped out, and whose creed of self-protection was "Let everything slide. For God's sake let everything slide."

So Queenie's notice was perforce accepted
and the squire's second day downstairs had
already the shadow of the registry office
over it.

Mrs. Limit, however, ruling in the kitchen,
was a grand woman. And Ruby liked her and
was not going to be shaken by Queenie's
defection. She had always thought Queenie
common, and she herself was all for the new
baby. The "Sister" upstairs had given it her
to carry into the garden once or twice. Ruby
was simple and rich-natured. A pity that the
squire had so little chance to know it. Queenie,
having given in her notice, was delighted with
herself, and thought she would try Leicester-
shire for a change. The household, for the
moment, ran a few paces by itself. Only Nurse
was growing a little restive for the midwife's
departure, and Nurse's girl muttered intermittently about the trays.

The two housemaids caused no trouble.
They sat much in their own rooms working
for a knitting competition, and spent long
afternoons knitting tassels into the woof and

web of two lilac jerseys. They were an excellent
pair and the squire would hardly have cared
that the house was not impeccable had not
Nurse pointed it out to her in one of her visits
to the library.

"Drat!" said the squire, immediately Nurse
began to speak.

"They've been idle since you've been upstairs," said Nurse. "Ask Mr. Pratt."

"Ho, I daresay!" said the squire. "He's
purely destructive. Who will lift a finger to
get others if these go?"

"Surely Mr. Pratt . . ." said Nurse hypo-
critically.

"You *know* he won't!" said the squire.

"I only want to help you," said Nurse. "In
other households the housemaids mix their
own beeswax."

"That's a fine point," said the squire.
"That's the unattainable!"

"Well, it's a queer friendship," said Nurse,
dropping her final seed. "And they haven't
their mind on their work."

The squire, infuriated, suddenly attacked

her. "The very second day I am down!" she
said. "A bit of dirt in the house can wait!
Nothing, nothing upsets me so much as these
hints of revolution, these hints of rumpus!"
She was hot, she felt like crying, her lip
trembled.

Nurse's childish kindness burst through her
wooden face and pale blue eyes. "Ah . . .
Tck . . . tck!" she said, vexed as vexed could
be. "It's only that I want the best for you.
And now I see it's not the best. It's having
you shut away these two weeks and not being
able to talk to you as I would like. And it's
wanting full charge that keeps me awake at
night."

Said the squire, wilfully misunderstanding
her, "Of the household?"

"Good gracious, no!" cried Nurse. "Of
him! And that girl in the nursery! I'm hoping
she'll change when *he* comes in to us, when
he's ours. But though I could I won't bring
you another worry! The girl's a queer girl.
It seems she's no heart. But I've said enough!"

"Better have it over now." (Queenie, the

housemaids, the nursery maid! The squire reeled.)

"I can't keep my words back, that's what it is! It's having no one to speak to in the nursery. I'm not happy about the petty cash. And two sixpences of Lucy's."

"Where do you keep the petty cash?"

"In the—— In my room."

"No, you keep it in the medicine cupboard!"

"Only very seldom. Only when I'm in a hurry."

"I've told you not to keep it in the medicine cupboard! It's a temptation to the girl. And as for Lucy's sixpences she doesn't deserve to have them. I found one in her shoe before I went to bed. You must never think things are stolen till the last ditch."

Nurse looked obstinate; the squire knew she had shelved nothing; she changed the subject, and spoke of Nurse's prince.

"Next Tuesday," she said. "I believe you'll have him next Tuesday."

"Is she going then? (Not that she isn't

wonderful!) But I can't keep my hands still till they get him. Boniface has got a tooth out, I meant to have told you."

"It came out?"

"No he pulled it out himself."

"That's a shilling then. Isn't it? One and six if it's taken out under gas. And sixpence if it just drops."

"That's right. He's coming down for it. Can he come now?"

"Send him now."

Nurse went. And fell over Boniface seated on the floor with his back to the door.

"Have you been listening?" She pushed him in, and went.

"Eaves," said Boniface, preoccupied.

"Eaves what?" said the squire.

"Dropping," he said, frowning a little and looking about.

"Why should you do that?"

"I left the . . ." he wandered round and round the room.

"What have you lost?"

"I left th' army an' navy——"

"What, *what?*"

"Catalogue."

(He has heard nothing, decided the squire. Better leave it alone.)

"What about your tooth?"

Boniface looked up brilliantly and curled back his lip. "I pulled it."

"That's a shilling," said the squire going over to her desk.

"I don't want it."

"Why ever not?"

"I DON'T WANT IT."

"But you want to buy something, don't you?"

"I DON'T want to buy something."

"Well," said the squire, returning from the desk without it. "There we are! If you don't."

"Here it IS! said Boniface, with a tremendous increase of voice, and picked up the Army and Navy Stores catalogue and went heavily down on the floor with it.

For three-quarters of an hour the squire listed and sorted her papers. To be answered, to be answered, to be answered, to be checked,

to be checked, account rendered, account
rendered, details requested, ninepence for wire
for temporary cook, fifteen shillings for fee
for temporary cook (to be disputed, to be
disputed), and behind her on the floor fluttered
the leaves of the catalogue and Boniface's
heavy black shoe tapped and tapped. She
glanced at the clock and grew restive. Could
he be reading, or was he simply resting his
brain against the well-thumbed pictures in the
catalogue? Ought she to allow him to let life
stand still like this?

"Boniface!"

He did not answer, doped above the slow-
moving pages.

"Stop reading a minute."

"Ow!" yelled Boniface instantly, dipping his
head and reading harder than ever.

The squire got up and went to the drawer
of another table. She had remembered a six-
penny purchase made before the baby's birth,
a paper packet of screws and bolts and bits of
metal that fixed together into a little trolley.
She dropped it beside the catalogue and

Boniface rolled an eye suspiciously on it; then he pushed the catalogue away and sat up. Still half in his trance he accepted the gift, opened the envelope and laid out the pieces; but while the squire read he did no more than arrange them for action.

"Aren't you going to put them together?" asked the squire.

"I can't seem to get going," murmured Boniface. Then he looked up, almost startled. "*You* know what it is!" he said briskly, as though his fog had been blown away by the thought. "*New* things I'm always sluggish at starting. *Aren't* I?"

"I believe you're partly lazy," said the squire, pondering.

"H'm." Boniface was unaffected by this.

The squire took a chance. They were so seldom alone together, he with his sudden look of being near her and alive to himself.

"You think too much, Boniface, you do too little. Look at the way you pretend these bits are put together, and you don't put them together. You put your hands in your pockets instead and pretend." He looked at her, waiting. "There was once a man," she said intently to him, reaching for an illustration to startle, "who was born without hands or feet . . ." Boniface sat slowly up and glared. "Born without hands or feet, but so wonderful, so determined, that he learnt to write, to ride, to paint."

"When?" said Boniface leaning forward.

"When what?"

"When did he die?"

"Die? He . . ."

"*When* did he die?"

"In 1889."

"Ouch . . . !" said Boniface, relaxing. "*That's* a good thing!"

"Why?"

"I shan't meet him. I'd be sick if I did."

The squire laughed at him and at herself. "Get on and screw up something!" she said.

"Who's that?" said Boniface, startled.

It was the window-cleaner again, inquisitive fellow, disturbing the morning.

"How long ago were you here?" asked the squire.

"A fortnight," said he.

"I've had my baby," she said, looking up.

"Yes, ma'am," said the window-cleaner.

"Wouldn't you——" said Boniface, and hung, unconcentrated and rambling.

"Wouldn't he what?"

"Wouldn't you have known?" he said, very loud, to the window-cleaner. The window-cleaner brought his little steps in over the window-sill without replying.

"It's very tiresome," thought the squire, "very tiresome. Why can't he ask before he comes? Padding round me, light-fingered little creature, watching my cheque-books and my keys and everything I have. I ought to send him away." But she was tired, the morning had been long and she was newly out of the midwife's protection. The thought of telling him to go turned her hot, though while he stayed she could not bear him.

Presently she noticed with annoyance that he was smoking.

"Don't you *know*," she burst out at him, "that you can't smoke in people's houses and clean their windows at the same time?"

"Pardon," said the little man, and carefully pressed out the end of his bit of cigarette and put it in a tin box. This made matters worse. Boniface was raising his head. In a minute he would make one of his comments.

"Have you any other windows to do?"

"Kep' these to the last," he said.

"Well you can leave them this morning. I'm busy. Telephone the house before you come next time."

He stepped away, catlike, with his ladder and his pail. She heard him whistle as he got to the corner of the wall.

"You were horrible," said Boniface.

"I feel horrible. He's a horrid little man."

"Oh," said Boniface, not really interested.

"It's lunch," said Nurse's girl, from the doorway.

"You can't get *my* shilling," said Boniface. There was silence.

"Because I haven't got it," he said.

CHAPTER THIRTEEN

It was the day of the midwife's departure. The squire went out into the garden and stood by the basket-cot. The ghost of a dream moved the baby; it gave a wondering, unearthly pipe and fell asleep again. All the links were snapping between the midwife and the baby. Yesterday he had cried in the garden and she did not go to him. Nurse popped her head apologetically in at the door.

"He's crying," she said uncertainly.

"Well go to him!" said the midwife with a smile, and made a gesture of her emptying hands. She had been there tense and waiting for his drama, had held him firm in the shock of birth, fended for him, settled his affair with his mother, now, her job over, she was prepared for another crescendo, ready for this great act again. Well, the squire was willing

216

and she laid her hand on the cot's brim. He and she were left. Between the midwife, the child and the squire the love-scene had passed and was over.

Nurse, bustling like a busy fowl in the nursery, a busy, happy fowl, rolled her eggs together and ruffled up the dust. She had put on a flannel apron with the dawn. It was her business to-day to bring the baby to his mother.

"It's part of my work," said the midwife, "to go. As much my work as it was to come."

The squire spoke slowly. "Do you regret him as I would regret him?"

"The baby?"

"The baby."

"My work here is finished," said the midwife. "Ten years ago I suffered at such partings. It is what we pay out for this profession of repressed maternity. No woman can assist at such a birth without a great wish to continue with the life of the child. Now I try not to give the babies love. I give my loving service to their welfare."

Through the evening they had talked

desultorily, with a sense of farewells, and the midwife slipped away before breakfast.

"Gone?" said the squire, staggered. And Nurse said, "She left this note."

"Take up the new day as though I had left last night," said the note. "Feed him at ten quietly, and read a book. You won't feel anxious or disturbed." To the last the mid-wife's mind was on the perfecting of her work, intent on slipping out without a ripple.

The squire took up a book at the breast-feed for the first time and began to read over the baby's head. He stared at the shadow, and when he was older he learnt to kick it down, but from now on the milk came mechanically and the squire's mind could range separately as it chose. From habit, as the days went by, like a cottage woman she grew bolder at her breast-feeds, and would walk from room to room, or give orders to Pratt over the baby's working head. She nursed him in the morning-room or in the garden, the children were allowed with her, the baby watched them out of one eye as he fed. He was unpacked now from his mystery and put into his family life.

Mrs. Limit would come in for orders, and sometimes Ruby was sent from the kitchen on a message. One morning she walked in while the baby fed. Her eyes shone and she said with a burst of feeling, "I wish *I* was nursery maid!" The squire looked thoughtful, knowing how Nurse felt about her girl. "I wish you could be," she said, rashly, and then qualifying, "But there's Minna."

"Minna's no good," said Ruby boldly. The squire would have liked to agree with her, but she distrusted these children of nature who ran to each other behind the scenes and swopped news. All she would say was, "You must wait. If there's a chance I'll give it to you."

And the chance came at once.

The baby back in his cot in the garden, the squire at her letters, her unending untidy household correspondence which washed up and down like the fret on the edge of the sea, she heard Nurse's step pounding through the hall.

"Boniface is sick," said Nurse in a hurry, and was off after fresh pyjamas to the hot-cupboard.

The squire went upstairs and along to Boniface's bedroom. He lay like a dead child, on his back, his arms by his side, the colour drained out of the mottle of his face, his lids flutteringly together.

"You want soda bicarbonate!" she cried.

"It's what I want," he murmured.

She brought him the tepid, nauseating mixture and he drank it at a swallow.

"Would you like something to read while you're getting better, or could you go to sleep?"

"I couldn't sleep. I couldn't read."

"Well I'll leave you. I expect you'll sleep."

"Hi . . ." he said rather louder, eyes still closed and colour faintly re-seated in the puffy cheeks.

"What?"

"I feel I could fiddle."

"Fiddle what with?"

"Your little letter-weighing-scales."

But when she brought the scales he had fallen asleep.

"What's he had?" said the squire to Nurse, passing from his room into the nursery.

"To *eat*, nothing!" said Nurse. "But there's been a scene." She got up with a tense face and shut the nursery door.

"I said to him, 'where's your watch'?" began Nurse, fast and low. "(It's just happened!) I said, 'where's your watch,' and *he* said, 'She keeps it in her suitcase'." And with that I went to her suitcase and pulled it from under her bed, and the girl started screaming. Boniface put his fingers in his ears and screamed too, 'stop it, stop it'."

"All this has just happened?" said the squire incredulously.

"It's all just happened and then Boniface was sick right there as he stood and I had to get him his pyjamas. Her suitcase is *full*. Full of silly things. Toilet-rolls and soap and honeycombs and broken toys. She must be dotty. She's sitting in her room and won't say another word."

"Better let me see the suitcase with my own eyes," said the squire, and walked into the room on the other side of the nursery.

There sat the nursery-maid, Minna, sunk into herself and glazed over with a dreary calm.

"What's this then, Minna?" said the squire. The girl made no answer; the suitcase lay in the middle of the room like a crime. The squire lifted the lid with her toe and saw the ridiculous collection. Pieces of chintz, bead-necklaces, an egg-cup, dish papers (two packets), a honey-comb (stove-in and leaking).

"What did you take these things for?"

Hopeless question! All the girl replied was, "I want to go home."

"Oh, you're going home all right!" said the squire grimly. "Did you take the petty cash too? Out of the medicine cupboard?"

"Not money I never! Things, but not money I never would!" said the girl with a flash of spirit.

"Well, never mind," said the squire. "I won't press it. Pull out these things, Minna, and lay them on the floor."

Slowly the girl crossed to the suitcase, knelt and did as she had been told. The odd medley was regimented on the linoleum.

"All these things are mine, you know," said the squire mildly, sitting in a chair and watching the unpacking. She had caught something regretful in Minna's eye as she set out her treasures.

"I've taken them," said Minna suddenly. "They're in my suitcase."

"Yes, but I've caught you," said the squire, "in time."

She sat and looked at Minna (vexed with herself). ("Half-baked, she is. Why can't I choose better? Why can't I know beforehand and avoid the bother and the trouble and the unpleasant relationships? Why can't I know a useless human being when I see it?") Aloud she said, "You'll be having your dinner in this room and going home this afternoon, Minna."

"That's whur I want to go!" said Minna passionately. "Mother'll know I'm no thief. I never took the money!" Hopeless! Infantile!

223

With the suitcase lying there before her on the
floor, full of stolen nonsense. Money or not
she was a thief, if that was the issue she was
going to bring up! But the squire saw the
point of the defence all the same. Money was
different. Money was over the borderline. And
in that defenceless kingdom from which Minna
came, with no reputation, no friends behind
her, the "money" accusation was a hoodoo, a
terror, sending one down-hill for ever, and
even the half-baked Minna had an instinct for
that. "Yes," Minna could say with her sullen
look, "I took your honeycombs and your
ribbons and your soap and your children's
toys, but your money I didn't take!" (But
she probably had all the same.)

Just send her home. That's all there was
to do. She had a loving mother evidently, who
believed in her, who was perhaps half-baked
too. Anyway the seed of that ludicrous suitcase lay deeper than the present. The poor
little magpie had got her picking fingers from
the past. She would find another little job after
a while and plod on. One couldn't waste time

reclaiming land that had no banks to keep the
sea out.

"Well, well, well," said the squire rising.
Minna said nothing, her eyes on the ground,
her ankles twisted round her chair-leg.

"What would you do, Nurse?" said the
squire, back in the nursery.

"Well, send her home I suppose," said
Nurse. "Send her home. Drat the girl."

"That's what I thought," said the squire.

Minna went home in the village car. With
Pratt, who much disliked his errand.

Nurse talked of her niece's second daughter,
but with misgivings. Her niece she had always
said was a pappy woman.

It was then that the squire spoke of Ruby,
presenting the idea with caution.

"Ah, if I could have *her!*" said Nurse. "A
real girl for children!"

So it was settled for Ruby, and the squire
wrote letters to registry offices about kitchen-
maids.

"You told the mother what had happened?"
said the squire to Pratt on his return.

Pratt grunted.

"What did she say?"

"She didn't appear to be very astonished, m'lady. She told the girl to get on in and have her tea."

Strange homes, strange backgrounds, a sad acceptance.

"And Minna? Was she upset?"

"The girl talked all the way home about the cat."

"The cat here?"

"No, her own cat, m'lady. It's all she thought of. That she'd see it again."

"Gosh!" said the squire, defeated.

CHAPTER FOURTEEN

I<small>T WAS PRATT'S HOLIDAY. HE SLID OUT</small> of their lives in August on a Wednesday. He did not say what he was going to do. "Where's he going?" said Lucy. "Ask him," said the squire. "I'd love to know."

"Where're you going, Mr. Pratt?" said Lucy.

"I've taken lodgings, Miss Lucy."

"Where?"

"Up near Manchester," said Pratt coldly. That was all they might know.

Crutchley came. Knowing his job, swift and fat, sliding through passages with a curious walk. He looked like a bald and nimble bishop, with a watch-chain where the cross should have lain. As he waited at table the watch ticked and Jay, on Sundays, could hardly help himself to cabbage.

"It's like the works of Crutchley's stomach."

"Mr. Crutchley smells sweet and cold," said Boniface.

"It seems like eau-de-Cologne," said the squire.

"He paints pictures," said Lucy. "He's painted the house."

"I saw him painting," said the squire. "Is it good?"

"A bit copyish," said Lucy.

"I thought it was good," said Jay.

Crutchley glided about at speed and seemed content and spoke a trifle frequently, very softly, very often. It was gay to have a let-up from Pratt's melancholy. The squire found herself shocked, and was shocked at herself for this. "It's as it should be," she consoled herself. "Pratt isn't human." She was constantly disloyal to Pratt in her relief at the change; but wondered what the servants' hall felt. Nobody said anything. "How do you like Crutchley, Nurse?"

"Well, it's only for a time."

* * * *

Jay and Lucy chalked Henry's nose red with
the squire's rouge-cake—his heated immature
nose. They worked with some eye-black found
almost dried in the squire's drawer, remains
and relics of her painted days. They took him
up the garden to the groom. But the groom
was out; the horses stared over the loose-box
doors. They took him to the Green, where
church was soberly disgorging through its
doors and gate, then abashed they turned and
went back into their own house, where the
squire and Boniface, passing through the hall,
saw them. Boniface, at sight of Henry's face,
fled, running up the garden path.

Henry giggled and worked his black eye-
brows up and down. He was compact and
horrible, old and old-fashioned, with his up-
turned black moustache.

"Take it off, you'll give him spots," said
the squire. "Why did you go out just as everyone was coming from church?" She looked at
Henry closer, with a pang. In a bound he had
reached the middle of his life, a little lady-
killer, a little showman, a little grown-up.

"My goodness!" said the squire to Lucy. "D'you think he'll grow up like that?"

"You are an awful little thing," said Lucy to Henry. Jay, bored, went up the path after Boniface.

"I've got someone coming to lunch," said the squire. "Clean up his face."

"Coming to *lunch!*" said Lucy indignantly. "Who's coming to lunch?"

"So I'm never to have anybody!" said the squire. "Go and cut the white roses from the top rose-bed. Cut them with the scissors that hang by the fireplace."

"Lucy eats her skin," said Henry, who was vexed with Lucy.

Lucy pushed him.

"She ate her skin at breakfast," said Henry.

"It was a scab," said Lucy. "I chewed it. So does everybody."

"Do they?" said Henry to the squire.

"Some time or other," said the squire absently. "Get him clean, Lucy. Not with soap. Use my face-cream. I'll cut the roses."

Boniface was wandering round the rose-bed when she arrived with the scissors.

"Where's Jay?"

"I dunno."

"Why did you run away?"

"I don't like . . ." said Boniface, his hands in his pockets, walking in circles.

"Hold the roses while I pass them over the hedge."

"They prick."

"Use your handkerchief."

"Don't!" said Boniface, "don't! I'm on my way . . ."

And he was gone, wherever his way was, walking by himself. That was motherhood, thought the squire, snipping at the stalks. Casual encounters about the garden and the house, with those on happy, secret errands. Glint in the eye, indication of a destination, feet running, a voice calling, a group loose-knit and close-knit, running at the end of faint elastic ropes, but tied still to her navel.

That was part of motherhood. Other landscapes to come, unseen, the blocked, silent future that made her wince. Ah, if she could carry this bundle of children with her into eternity, clutched to her breast, with iron arms like God's. "But the navel strings will wear fine and break and each will go out to found its family and sow its seed." What is personality, where does it go? So childish, so fundamental, so useless, so wild a question.

But she must get ready for the woman who was coming to lunch. There never seemed, as she looked through her cupboard, to be a dress that was suitable.

Ready at last, she was down in time to lift Boniface's black toad-like shoes from the middle of the drawing-room carpet. The guest arrived, they had sherry, and went in. The squire dismissed Crutchley, saying they would help themselves. She was aware that this was a confidential luncheon, that now she had to listen to the complications of love.

The visitor was stretched pleasantly on her emotional rack when the door opened and Nurse carried in the baby for his two o'clock feed—the squire, as her face lit at sight of him,

perfectly aware of the annoyance he would
cause to the speaker. But the baby, she must
have the baby! The baby couldn't miss his
lunch for anybody's lover! The Confider,
staggering momentarily in her tale, paused and
tried to admire the baby. "But go on!" said
the squire. "I've got to nurse him. He makes
no fuss. Go on."

With her lover in her lap she listened to the
visitor telling of hers. Love all at once seemed
to the mother indescribably stale.

The baby choked, and the story was pulled
up with a jerk. The squire shook him gently.
"Go on," she said over his head, and so the
love clanked on, grinding in its cogs. When
the baby had been taken away the light went
out of the room. That emptied vase which
was the mother turned again to her visitor
"She thinks I am a woman fit to listen to love,"
she thought, and listening with abstracted
effort, cupped her chin in her hand.

When the guest had gone she remembered
a box of seedlings that had arrived; and pulling
off the mistaken dress she fled to the garden,

engulfed soon in that murmurous happiness,
spooning in earth round the roots, crouching
and listening to the noise of bees, her square
hands pushing and pressing, her thoughts
floating like silk, the back of the brain, un-
troubled, bursting into flower.

"Where's Jay?" she wondered (suddenly
wondering "Where's Jay?").

This she would do at odd moments in the
flight of the day, as a bird looks under its
breast on the nest to count once more its
clutch of eggs. "Where's Jay? Where's
Henry? Lucy? Boniface?"

Jay like Boniface had his own hard-working
private life. Jay filled in coupons and received
each morning a post from people who sent
him samples of toothpaste, lip-salve, Lactagol,
staples, and once a rubber contraption which
the squire, in a burst of courage and resolu-
tion, explained to him. (But he forgot again.)

He seemed to have endless money saved
from Christmas and invested in the Post Office,
out of which he bought his own stamps and
wrote postcards cooped up in his bedroom on

a hot day with the windows shut.

She called him now; but with his windows shut as usual he could not hear. She called louder, and the fair head was thrust out. "D'you want me?"

"Whatever you're doing bring it down!"

"Ink an' all?"

"I've got ink here."

He came down slowly carrying all his needs. Catalogues, postcards, stamps in an envelope, his special pen, and blotter.

"I never see you," said the squire, explanatory. "Can't you write on the table under the tree?"

"Are you going to garden?"

"Yes, a bit."

"Good." With method, he installed himself, bringing out her ink from the morning-room, and the silence in the garden was unbroken as Jay wrote steadily and stuck on stamps and the squire pressed the earth in round her little plants.

It was then he looked up and could not see her. The garden went cold.

"Where are you!" he called so sharply she was startled.

"Behind the tree" (putting her head round, stooped upon her knees). And she saw the beautiful face smooth out as he relaxed again, like a horse that has been patted.

Navel strings, navel strings, when would they break? Perhaps never. Perhaps one day, looking back from eternity, she would see that there had never been anything to fear.

But in two minutes she was cross with him. He was crumpling up unsatisfactory letters and throwing them on the grass. That, really, was beyond a joke! She flamed with indignation, and, unperturbed at her scoldings, he fetched the waste-paper basket. See-saw, see-saw, went life, and the ups and downs of the heart.

"Hey! Boniface!" called Jay, hearing the scuff of naked feet. Boniface walked on. "Boniface, Boniface, hi!" Boniface went up the path, thinking hard, lurching thoughtfully. Jay was after him, scattering his pen and paper. Boniface began to run.

"Napoleon, Napoleon . . ." gasped Jay.

"He's just behind the hedge—there, in front! He'll get you!"

Boniface screamed and turned and rushed the other way.

"He's dodged!" shouted Jay. "He's got round! He'll get you there too. Look out, Boniface!"

Boniface threw himself on the ground shrieking, destroying the air and the calm and the garden with fear.

The squire, upright on her knees, watched, puzzled. Jay sauntered back.

"What's this?" she said, frowning uncertainly.

"He likes it," said Jay. "You'll see. He's coming back for more."

And there was Boniface approaching, a wide, half-frightened grin dawning on his face.

"You can't see him!" teased Jay, "but he's standing behind me . . . Pounce! Look out! He'll be out!"

"Nelson!" said Boniface faintly, trying to reassure himself.

"Nelson's no good. He's got no pounce. Shall I go upstairs and get the bust?"

"No, no."

"I think I will."

"No! No . . . no . . ."

"Stop it, Jay!" said the squire. "What's he frighened of Napoleon for?"

"It's that little tin bust in my room, the one I bought at the Tomb in Paris. He half pretends he's taken a horror of it. We spring it at him."

"D'you mind, Boniface?"

"I don't," said Boniface, eyeing the shadow behind Jay nervously.

"He likes it. He always comes for more," said Jay.

"Well stop it now," said the squire, still on her knees.

Jay went back to his coupons; Boniface, his original intention broken up, brought a large pink book from the morning-room and laid himself along a wooden seat.

"Jay, I'm getting tired of that coupon-filling."

"Oh . . ." said Jay deprecatingly, continuing to write.

"It's a waste of time, it crowds the hall table with parcels, it's a waste of your money. We don't give you your money at Christmas for that."

"But you give it for me, don't you?"

"To do something sensible with."

"No, to do something that makes me happy."

"That *can't* make you happy."

"It makes me frightfully happy."

He licked an envelope and placed a stamp on it.

"Who taught you not to lick the stamps?"

"Nurse," said Jay. "Lucy licks hers."

"She doesn't write any letters."

"She would if she did. She likes the taste."

"Eats her scabs, eats her scabs!" said Boniface, reading and kicking the seat.

"Gar!" said Jay. "That's Henry's joke."

Now Henry joined them, passing up to his "rest" at the top of the garden.

"I've got five minutes," said Henry.

239

"Go away," said Boniface, his face in his book. "I can't read."

"You're reading, aren't you?" said Henry coldly. He dawdled up to the squire.

"Shall I help you? I've got five minutes."

"Don't give them to me. They're too precious!"

"I'd *love* to give them to you," said Henry, his face shining. But he jumped away to Jay, forgetting his offer.

Nurse appeared in the garden doorway.

"That's not five minutes! That's not five minutes!" roared Henry, and burst into tears.

So, talking, sticking on stamps, kneeling with a trowel by the flower-bed, the afternoon shadows grew longer and the hours went by. Henry, who had long been taken to his rest, came down again, a rose in his hand.

"You're not to pick the roses!" said the squire.

"It fell off!" said Henry shocked.

"I beg your pardon, Henry."

Crutchley brought her tea-tray into the courtyard. The squire rose to pour out a

cup, and picked up the pink book that Boniface
had let fall. It was the annual drug report from
Egypt, and stuck to its cover was a piece of
soft putty from the builder's yard. The squire
sniffed the cool lump. She may have exhausted
the pleasures of youth but she had never
forgotten them. Putty! Could a piece of putty
with its unexplainable smell leave any old
man unmoved?

*   *   *   *

Crutchley on arrival had seized the flower-
doing out of the squire's hands, and liked to
erect a "massif" in the dining-room. The
squire winced and thought—"it's only for a
time!"

On Saturday following the luncheon it was
hot and still. Crutchley was in and out
gathering fig-leaves to put under the fruit.
He had found some wire-netting and crumpled
it up in the flower-bowl so that the flowers on
the dining-room table stood up like the back
of a hedgehog. The squire, passing the open
dining-room door, sniffed. "Well, it's only

for a time!" she thought. He was full of initiative, with fat, flexible hands, and a silky taste.

"Lunch at one," she said to Queenie, next day, as she passed through the hall. On Sundays the children all came down to lunch. "Tell Crutchley. Perhaps he doesn't know."

Queenie vanished, with a look on her face.

"Nurse!" called the squire up the nursery stairs. "Boniface wants cleaning. I've just seen him. He's been to the stables."

Boniface came down, smiling, from the garden above.

"It's only manure," he said as he heard her call.

"Manure," said Jay, walking behind him and holding his nose. "It's rotten bird."

When lunch-time came they were all clean and sat round the table even before the sounding of the gong. Nurse, who usually came down with them, preferred (now that she had to get the baby up in time for his two o'clock feed and prepare him) to have her lunch early, sent from the servants' hall.

Queenie brought in the egg-and-mushroom soufflé.

"We're here!" called Lucy. "The first course is in!"

Queenie stood to attention by the open door of the dining-room waiting for the squire. The children sat in the draught waiting. The squire's clean napkin blew down onto the floor, a rose fell out of the bowl, the dish steamed while the squire rinsed her hands under the tap. She came in shaking them dry, sat down hurriedly and picked her napkin from the floor. "Go on, Queenie. Where's Crutchley?"

"He's not quite ready, m'lady."

Oddnesses of Crutchley, little slips and softnesses. Not ready on Sunday! Henry's face was a clean pearl, his napkin tucked beneath. Boniface rosy and brushed, eyes rolling on the dish, Jay and Lucy quiet and hungry. The dish went round.

"Do you like this, Boniface?"

"I don't," said Boniface.

"You liked it up to last Sunday," said Jay.

"Then I've changed my mind," said Boniface.

Lucy looked towards the door. Queenie seemed strangely insufficient, the room half-empty without Crutchley. Boniface fiddled with the glass mustard-pot that ran on gilded wheels.

The door opened silently and Crutchley came in, crossed to the table and hovered near the squire. An overwhelming smell of eau-de-Cologne poured down upon her. Boniface's round eyes stared at him behind the squire's head with an animal's bright glare. The squire sniffed and looked at him. At that he bowed deeply, and a dank lock of hair fell across his smoking forehead. He was very hot.

"You can take away their plates, Crutchley. I shall have finished in a moment."

Crutchley moved about, tiptoeing oddly. Queenie removed the plates.

Both disappeared with the trays and the door shut on them.

"What's the matter with Crutchley?"

244

whispered Lucy, breathing hard and leaning towards her mother.

"Nothing," said the squire, with extraordinary firmness. "He's not well. If you say one word, Boniface, you'll eat your meat in the nursery."

Unusual burst of severity! The children stared. Crutchley and Queenie returned, Queenie carrying the joint, and the meal went on. "You must hurry," said the squire to the children. "I must be ready for the baby at ten minutes to two."

"It's nowhere near ten to two," said Lucy.

"Mr. Crutchley's drunk," said Boniface, firm and loud.

Crutchley made no response. If indeed he heard at all. Jay and Lucy, with frightened faces, bolted sirloin and Yorkshire pudding. Crutchley bowed and minced, altering and re-altering the positions of cutlery, a shadow butler in his own shadow world. The meal finished the squire withdrew her silent children and they went into the courtyard for coffee. Slowly Crutchley descended the four steps to the courtyard with the silver tray, steadily poured the coffee into her outstretched cup, turned from her, placed the tray on the courtyard table, and going back to the dining-room, passed away from consciousness in the squire's own chair.

Here, from the door, the squire surveyed him, called at last by Queenie to her help—Queenie, who, in a mysterious loyalty, had borne much. The squire looked from the door mutely and with interest.

"Would the gardeners be in? It's Sunday."

"Just after lunch they'd be in, m'lady."

"You get them, Queenie. And get his bed ready. You think he'll stay asleep all the afternoon?"

"He'll sleep till dinner-time," said Queenie.

"Then we must be ready what to do by dinner-time. Why didn't you tell me before?"

"I thought your ladyship knew."

"Good God," said the squire.

The gardeners dragged Crutchley to his bed, undressed and settled him in. He lay like a a baby, flushed and snoring slightly. The squire went to Mrs. Limit for enlightenment.

"Terrible it's been," said Mrs. Limit. "What's to be the end of him?"

"Mrs. Limit, I don't care!" said the squire. "I'm not going to reclaim him. He goes to-morrow morning with a week's wages, and board."

"Well, that's very generous, he can't complain."

Crutchley went with a mildness and a lack of expostulation that showed the habitual exit, melting, suitcase in hand, the week's wages and board in his pocket. They managed with Queenie alone, and the under-housemaid helped. The maids seemed drawn together by Crutchley's fall. Pratt came back at the end of his holiday and resumed his melancholy reign. The subject of Crutchley did not come up until a few days after Pratt's return; and then the squire spoke of it casually in the warmth of dinner-time by candlelight, the night blue and airy behind the candles and the open window.

"Ah," said Pratt, the rare look coming on to his face, "he's one of *them*. A bottle and a quarter he could manage, I daresay." He spoke as though he were speaking of his old regiment.

"What of?" said the squire.

"Whisky," said Pratt. "Cheapest and quickest."

"What'll happen to him then?"

"He'll die," said Pratt.

The squire gloomed into the candles, her thoughts fastened with a shiver to the flames, looking after Crutchley into what was now already the past. The old vice, to disintegrate the flesh with spirit, with potatoes, with rye, throughout history, alcohol, the immortal companion of man—like his wife, like his dog—alcohol the counterblow to the weight and loneliness of life, the low explosive that broke up the day's prison and lit it with a combustion of mellow gases. She had not the slightest inclination to go after him and drag him from his death, but watched him in the candle-flame and thought of death, her own, his, one way or another, sooner or later. It really was his own affair. Pink and swift and

like a bishop, it was his own affair. Strange
how we appear in the world, with an *appearance*
for a time. Crutchley to look like Crutchley,
and Pratt like Pratt, moulded and painted and
passing away.

It had been the children's subject for days,
talking of it, acting it, relating it again to Nurse.
Nurse was vexed that she had been absent.
What a Sunday lunch! The children had lived
through something.

"But why was Boniface the only one who
knew?" said Nurse for the hundredth time.

"How did you know, Boniface?"

"He looked giddy," said Boniface and
smiled, well-pleased.

"What'll happen to him?"

"He won't live long," said Nurse, as a
lesson to Jay.

"Couldn't he be helped?" said Lucy.

"Not worth while," said the squire who was
passing through the nursery. This was as a
lesson to Lucy, to close her heart a little. To
show her that in the world there were irre-
claimable things, wastage of time, and life.

Mother could say, could she, that in the world there were certain acts that were not worth doing, even though they involved death? Mother was tough. But mother was *not* tough. That was the lesson. Such things brushed Lucy on the understanding and on the spirit.

But these were higher moments. Usually they played drunks and Jay acted Crutchley, tiptoeing about and bowing. It was revolting.

"That's enough," said Nurse.

"Let 'em play it out," said the squire, feeling obscurely that this was for the children's good. "Sausages and drunks. Harlequinade for the nursery."

"I think we've had enough of it," said Nurse.

"Wait till *they* have."

Nurse did not think the squire so peculiar as she used to think her, for during the course of time she would come a little under her sway. It was only after the August holiday, when Nurse went home, that she reverted and came back, not hostile, but tightened and inelastic.

Long before Christmas she was tuning in again with the squire.

"How's Ruby?" said the squire.

"Shaping," said Nurse.

The squire, who had spoken casually, drew a breath of relief and went downstairs. Ah, this old feudal nonsense in a toppling world! Nonsense and a trouble but it had to go on. No other way of living if you wanted to walk to your grave cloaked in the English life.

CHAPTER FIFTEEN

THE TRAVELLER HAD SAILED. HE WAS already on the sea. There was time but for one more letter to be written to Marseilles.

His room doors were set wide open, his Indian rugs hung sunning on wall and branch, Pratt had polished the wine filter and was making up his cellar book.

The squire came down late one morning and passed across the hall to order the meals. The children were nowhere; the house was quiet and dim and full of summer; Mrs. Limit stifled a yawn as the squire entered the kitchen.

"Have we all overslept?" said the squire. "I have."

"Terribly heavy last night," said Mrs. Limit.

"At last, at last," breathed the squire, "I can

rest in the bosom of my cook," and she sank into the wooden chair and took up the slate with the chalk writing upon it.

"They've brought in a bit of asparagus," said Mrs. Limit.

"The children . . ." began the squire.

"Just enough for your ladyship's dinner," said Mrs. Limit.

Even at this hour of the morning the squire's juices flowed.

Boniface put his red face in at the kitchen door.

"My bit of dough?" he said to Mrs. Limit.

"Boniface!" asked the squire. "Would you like a special pudding?"

"Friday's fish day," he said.

"What's that got to do with it? I said 'pudding'."

"When we have fish we have suet," said Boniface.

"But you told me you hated suet. Wouldn't you like something else?"

The eager look which his face had worn was lost and his lip dropped.

"I'd better keep to my routine," he muttered. "I'd better."

"But . . ."

"Don't keep on!" he said. And fled, without his dough.

"Well!" said Mrs. Limit.

"He likes safety," said the squire. "He sticks like a limpet to his old rock!"

"An' he hates that suet!" said Mrs. Limit.

"He'd rather eat it than be prised off it," said the squire.

Sleep had not sweetened Pratt. She found him in his shirt-sleeves in the pantry ironing the evening trousers that waited on her at night. He stood back, iron in hand, and the smoke rose from the trousers. The cupboard doors of his silver and china stood open, revealing the litter within. Stale knobs of sugar, pipes, a melting butter-pat in a saucer, the silver kettle with the handle newly off. Silently closing the cupboard doors with her hand the squire turned to speak to him. It was a gesture which held a truce in it. "We have fought over that cupboard enough," said her hand, "we will never speak of it again."

Queenie, who had taken back her notice, bustled in as the squire was coming out of the pantry, then stood back to allow her to pass.

"Ruby says the baby's crying, m'lady!"

"He'll cry himself off," said the squire placidly. "He's just been put down."

"Cool, ain't she!" said Queenie to Pratt when the squire had gone.

"Knows her job," said Pratt in a deep rumble, glaring at Queenie.

Back in the library the letters and bills were strewn, half-sorted, but Lucy came in and hung over the writing-table.

"What are you doing?" said the squire, dipping her pen in the ink.

"Nothing."

"Why are you here?"

"To talk to you."

"What about?"

"Nothing."

They smiled at each other.

So they talked; and the squire suddenly

abandoned her letters, took a weeding fork and went out into the garden, Lucy following her. The little weeds popped up onto the hot brick path and wilted. The squire shook the earth out of their roots before she laid them down.

"Get the hearth brush from in there and you can brush the earth back into the border."

Lucy brushed and the squire finicked up the weeds so that the tube of root remained intact. The moment was full of peace; but peace was not enough, beauty was not enough; Lucy spoke of her only trouble.

"How old are you?" she said.

This passage always there, this passing always felt, this movement of the rope along and the hands laid on it as we pace beside it (desperate and beautiful life!). While the squire pulled out a flat weed she was beside herself with pity for humanity. This short, this fearful loveliness, in which men and women, heroic and baffled, struggling to wisdom, age as they struggle; wrestle upwards and drop into the ground. This marriage, this association

256

with matter, what a high-handed experiment, but what admirable victims! Man, with his eye on death, draws his foot from the womb. There is not time for anything, yet there is time for everything. No sooner appreciate love than skin withers, no sooner grow wise than we are unfit for wisdom. Learning to live and defeated by death. Discovery succeeds discovery, and nothing accumulates. We live haunted. We grasp and grasp; what we hold dissolves, our very hands dissolve.

"But," thought the squire, "what an invention for pleasure and for pain! Behind me my life strings out,—efforts, triumphs, astonishment, days and nights of living, ready to be called back, remembered and caressed. Many thousand wakings full of hope and delight. Comfort, anticipation, greed, when the body, snuggling into warmth, or bending over food, calls down the spirit like a dog and bids it attend in the bedchamber. And those moments too I would not have forgone, for when again on my everlasting journey shall I know this visitation of matter, this inhabiting of sentient, dissolving, iridescent stuff, this 'at-home-ness', this living at once cosy and terrible, those two divinities fame and love—those two divinities food and warmth?"

The squire looked at her little girl and thought of her deep heart, her keen intelligence. But does it matter how one is equipped for the battle? The battle is lost before it is begun. Whatever your armour it all goes, lances and spears and breastplates.

"I am forty-four," she said.

"That's nothing, is it?"

"Hardly the middle of life," said the squire.

Lucy, restless and appeased, heard a stable dog howl at the clang of the Convent bell, and went off, dropping her brush.

"Put the brush back!" shouted the squire, cross at once.

"When I come back!" called Lucy, beginning to run.

The squire, hot with anger, raised herself and called after her. Lucy returned.

"When you take a thing out——" began the squire, and abused the reincarnation of her own untidy self. Faults that were her own she would not have. Lucy, unflurried, took back the brush to the room whence she had brought it. This was how she preferred her mother, for now she felt life more solid. Silences in which the spirit bloomed made her uneasy. The brush returned she went up to the stable.

But now the squire had woken the baby. He began to scold and grumble and practise his voice in his cot behind the apple trees. He heard her movements and arched his back, standing on his head and his heels and looking over the top of his forehead. Hot from sleep but alive his arms worked like a windmill. Soaking the shawl he lay on he grew chilled and began to cry. The squire rose and walked behind the espaliered trees to his cot. The cries stopped, his eyes glittered; not a tear shone in them and rage was wiped out like a dream. She pulled him from his cot and his head ducked onto her shoulder. The red, creased buttocks clenched and unclenched like a fist, the knees climbed her breast. She bent and rested the baby lightly on the grass, bare

to his armpits where his garment had risen
in a fold. His curled feet hardly touched the
ground, the unworn coral toes sought for a
substance, found the grass and the earth, spoke
to it, gently tapping it, and then in shy delight
retracted back into the safe and unsubstantial
air. Again and again the toes came down,
alternate feet taking a fraction of the weight of
the body, the unused foot scraping the standing
leg.

She plucked him up, smoothed down his
vest, and tucked him in his cot. As she moved
behind him she was gone out of his vision
like the sun falling out of the sky. The flag
of rage ran up on the knotted forehead, eyes
were lost in creases, he caught his breath,
choked, bellowed, rent the air. All the birds
hushed in the trees as the cry came.

When he ceased screaming time stood still.
The squire heard him shuffle, catch his breath,
sigh, and there was silence. Peering through
the apple leaves she saw his lids at half-mast,
between sleeping and waking, arm abandoned
above his head, fingers scattered, she closed

her eyes lest the weight of her glance should
burn him, her will hard against his. And he
slept. She crept away.

*   *   *   *

The day passed and evening came. The
children now developed a feverish gaiety, life
snatched in double strength before sleep. The
sun sank and extraordinary lights played in
the garden. Henry made a bonfire in a flower-
pot, Boniface tricycled round the paths, Jay
carried a short ladder here and there, and Lucy
followed her mother, talking and talking.
Wherever the squire went there was Lucy
talking.

"Go and help Henry," said the squire.

"He doesn't want help," said Lucy.

"I don't want help," said Henry.

"And have you noticed . . ." said Lucy.
Lucy's mind lit up in the evening like Henry's
bonfire. Fiercer and fiercer grew her hold on
life between Henry's bedtime at six and her
own at seven. "So have you noticed . . ."
said Lucy, lighting and flashing as the sun sank.

The squire said to herself, "The newness, the *newness* of their conversation! Who would want contemporaries!"

One after the other the knell of the four bedtimes struck. While the squire was nursing the baby Henry went, saying angrily that his fire wasn't out. Then went Boniface, reading as he walked. They disappeared at intervals of a quarter of an hour. The bath could hardly fill and empty quickly enough. Boniface often had Henry's water. Lucy found a thousand excuses but went at last. Now the squire could hear her own bath running before dinner.

The garden was empty. Too early for stars but not too early for sherry. Pratt brought it and put it on the table under the tree. The stable tabby was mating and flitting in the bushes, with black shadow and brown shadow and piebald. There would be a moon to-night. The bath-water from the nursery bubbled down the waste-pipe, unseen but marking the stages. Soon there would be cups of milk and fruit salad round the nursery table.

The squire sat upright on a bench in the

garden, vigorous but stilled, her square hands spread on her full lap, sipped her sherry, knew her bay of peace and that the tempest howled outside. Europe and the future, sickness, accident, dispersal and age rode like gaunt ships upon the breakers. But now she was allowed by time, by chance, her peace, her idleness. Nursing her baby she had a right to her quiet. She stared and saw nothing, not the flat planes of grass, not the lightless walls. The little glass of sherry cast her loose from her garden seat. The walls of her home became glass. Bricks and mortar and blood and bone liquefied and broke up, dissolved. Under Father Sun at midday, under the wild phenomenon of the moon at night she saw herself crouched with her litter, a pyramid of birth, a pheasant over its young under the Great Hawk's eye.

Thinking in waves of emotion from her heart she said low,—"We get over all desires. Even love, even affection, even this passion for the children. Ceasing, ceasing to want things. Joining the procession." She took her place then in a line of women like a figure on a roll of film, her mother before her, her children behind, in a dream, in a bubble, in a fever, in an incandescence of oxygen and salt and water, that beautiful display called life. "Lucy," whispered the squire, and had an odd sense that Lucy was herself, that she herself was her own mother, that these three women were one.

And with a deep, female pride, she felt herself an archway through which her children flowed; and cared less that the clock in the arch's crown ticked Time away.

Down the steep hillside beyond the confines of the garden came the evening sheep, scattering and crowding as they moved, oozing by the scar of the chalk-pit like white lice from a white wound. They wept. The day was going from them. An old miserable cry swept from end to end of the flock. But as they moved they ate and their meal was ceaseless through their immemorial woe.

Nurse, on her way to put the cat-net on the baby in the garden, stood a moment to listen to the sheep. "How they cry," she said. Her face was square and happy; her work filled her life. That her baby was borrowed and would grow and leave her, was nothing to her. Some live in to-day some in to-morrow, and nurse's life was in to-day. She stood and watched the sheep, then with a rustle passed on with the net in her hand, and through the apple trees her white figure padded.

When she came back the squire had gone; gone to her bath. And after the bath and before dinner—good nights. Henry, Boniface, Jay and Lucy. Henry was asleep.

"Boniface," whispered his mother cautiously as she passed his window on the balcony. "You've come *too late!*" said Boniface. "I'm settled. I'm asleep. Don't unsettle me!" Sometimes he chose to face the night without a farewell.

"Jay . . ."

The pink curtains at his window with the pale green donkeys on them swung gently, half-drawn. The squire drew them even further back and looked down onto the Green. Jay read, his shining hair brushed for the night. "Oh, Jay," she said, "I hope you have a lovely life."

"I hope so, too," he said, and looked awed.

To Lucy she entered with a firm look. Introspection at bedtime, remorses for the day's shortcomings, a little scene, a little intimacy—these would be offered up and had to be avoided. The room was apple-green and square and nearly dark.

"Put on the light!"

"No, you're all settled, stay like that!"

"How I hate sleep!"

"Now, Lucy!"

Lucy had bad dreams. An owl came to the window and she thought it was a soul. Sometimes she would scream in her sleep as though her throat were being cut. Henry had bad dreams, too. Jay never dreamt. Boniface never dreamt. Why was this? From what pockets of heredity came these children?

Lucy would not have books left in her room at night, lest something should crawl out from the cover. Worst of all this night the squire left *Hamlet* lying by the child's bed when she was called to the telephone. She found the book flung through the door when she returned.

"Really, really . . ." a little impatiently.

"The ghost in Hamlet," whispered Lucy lying with knotted face in her bed.

So the squire gave in and said no more. But Lucy was alive and ready to talk, lit as with alcohol (but with fears).

"Have I been good enough? Have I been grateful enough?" (World-pain aching like a bad tooth.)

"Grateful? What for?"

"Everything. You, you," mumbled Lucy, with a stiff look, afraid of response, afraid of confession.

"Lucy!" said the squire, remembering all her girlhood. "Don't get that pain at your heart about what I do for you, that tenderness, that kind of anguish! Shake free from that while you can. I, too, used to have it about my mother. And now that I'm your mother I see it wasn't needed, it had no need to be there.

Can you understand when I tell you that you owe me nothing? That to have a child is an account which is settled on the spot?"

Lucy kept her fixed look, not understanding but waiting for the words to clear.

"Love me but don't be grateful. I'm paid by having you. And what I do for you I do for myself! See, when I scold you I don't love you less, and when I give you presents I don't love you more! My pride in you is my own vanity. You are myself, Lucy, you children are my family, my future, my skin. If I were starving and fed you it would be I who received the food!"

"Yes, . . ." said Lucy labouring with her thoughts.

The squire waited.

"What children *can't* understand," said Lucy slowly, "is the *way* parents love their children."

"It comes like an appetite!" said the squire briskly and gaily, closing the pores on Lucy's inner skin like cold water after a bath. "Till the food is there you don't know what it tastes

268

like." And peacefully Lucy was cast into the night like a fish which is slid without a splash into a pond.

Night closed down upon the household and lights were lit.

Nurse, Pratt, the maids, the children, were away mysterious, alone. Pratt must be reading somewhere, the window-cleaner could not now come on his ladder, the last post was in. Nurse had her cap off, and was burning her kidneys with her back to the fire.

It was nearly ten. Out stole the squire into the burning garden, the silver garden. Stars pointed and leapt. She crept to the summer house, dipped her head with memories of ten years of bumps on the too-low roof, and feeling her way to the cot, loosed the tight net that kept the cats away. Then felt for the baby and dragged him out, shawls, steaming damp, wound round him. His forehead lay in her neck and his knees rose against her. He was assuming, in his disturbed sleep, his pre-natal position. Nurse's steps could be heard on the stone flags round the corner of the house.

The squire dodged into the morning-room door and shut it after her. While nurse in her turn felt her way to the now-empty cot the squire unwrapped the cocoon and its arms flew above its head in an almighty stretch. It sneezed, yawned, wrinkled. It woke. And was immediately hypnotized by the flames of the summer fire.

"Have you got him?" Nurse opened the morning-room door and stood in the doorway, framed by that sky. Through Nurse's hairs it winked, stars, twigs, and hairs.

The baby popped his head round and smiled. Then made a face, savouring the acidities of sleep. Fed, Nurse took him, and he sailed like a king out of the room, and the squire was left alone.

Picking up a pad of paper by her side where she still sat in the corner of the sofa, long she wrote to catch the ship at Marseilles, her final weekly chronicle, her last report of the children and his home.

Night closed more deeply down and lights were put out. Outside the black sky opened wider and showed by its signals its immensities. The squire's village, her white house, black windows, rolled with the rest of the world among the wheels and geometrical terrors of heaven.

THE END

The first Virago Modern Classic was published in London in 1978, launching a list dedicated to the celebration of women writers and to the rediscovery and reprinting of their works. While the series is called "Modern Classics" it is not true that these works of fiction are universally and equally considered "great," although that is often the case. Published with new critical and biographical introductions, books appear in the series for different reasons: sometimes for their importance in literary history; sometimes because they illuminate particular aspects of women's lives, both personal and public. They may be classics of comedy or storytelling; their interest can be historical, feminist, political, or literary. In any case, in their variety and richness they promise to confuse forever the question of what women's fiction is about, while at the same time affirming a true female tradition in literature.

Initially, the Virago Modern Classics concentrated on English novels and short stories published in the early decades of the century. As the series has grown, it has broadened to include works of fiction from different centuries and from different countries, cultures, and literary traditions; there are books written by black women, by Catholic and Jewish women, by women of almost every English-speaking country, and there are several relevant novels by men.

Nearly 200 Virago Modern Classics will have been published in England by the end of 1985. During that same year, Penguin Books began to publish Virago Modern Classics in the United States, with the expectation of having some 40 titles from the series available by the end of 1986. Some of the earlier books in the series were published in the United States by The Dial Press.